D0282478

The Grand Leader

The Grand Leader

A YARN BY

Armis E. Hawkins

For Martha,
Enjoy!
Warm Regards,
Jim

J Prichard Morris Books
Jackson, Mississippi

This is a work of fiction.
Names characters, places, and events are products of the author's
imagination, or they are used fictiously
for authenticity. Any resemblance to actual
persons, living or dead, events, or locales
is entirely concidental.

Copyright © 2007 by the family of Armis E. Hawkins

Drawings by Dale Hawkins Carr

All rights reserved
This book, or any parts therof, may not be
reprinted in any form without permission of the publisher.

J PRICHARD MORRIS BOOKS
801 Arlington Street,
Jackson, MS 39202
601 354-9716

ISBN 978-0-9708047-3-0

Library of Congress Control Number: 200793703

Printed in the United States of America
FIRST EDITION

This is a yarn—
nothing more, nothing less.

The geographical area of Mississippi
known as the Flatwoods
bears faint resemblance to the
Flatwoods at the time
of this story.

A.E.H.

CONTENTS

PUBLISHER'S NOTE

Armis Hawkins and I began talking about the possibility of publishing *The Grand Leader* five or six years ago. He had recently retired as chief justice of the Mississippi Supreme Court after a long and distinguished law career. Noted for the literary quality of his legal writings, he had never before written a novel. Our mutual friend, Jo Haxton—known in the literary circles as the acclaimed writer Ellen Douglas—had read an early draft and thought it was worthy of publication. She asked me if I could help him get it into publishable form and explore publishing possibilities. I found its conversational style and quirky characters enchanting, and I enthusiastically agreed to work with him.

Armis was adamant about the importance of preserving the pronunciation and speech of north Mississippi hill people of the 1930s and wanted to retain as many of the phonetic spellings as possible. Yet the dialect occasionally got in the way of the story. My friend Carol Cox, a sensitive reader and a fine copyeditor, helped us find a way to eliminate some of the dialect yet still enable the reader to "hear" the way characters spoke. We decided to keep most of the phonetic spellings in the dialogue but use more conventional spelling in the first person narration. Idiosyncratic regional grammatical usage, speech patterns, and word choices from the period would remain intact throughout. This means that occasionally a racial epithet occurs in the book, just as it commonly did in the conversation of some Mississippians in the 1930s. Armis Hawkins himself was not a racist and did not condone the use of the objectionable epithet.

I sent the copy edited manuscript to Armis to review and make final revisions. By the time he received it in 2005, he had become very ill, and we were unable to proceed for several months. Not long before his death in February 2006, however, he finished going over the manuscript and made notes for a few additional changes. It would be more than a year later that his son, Jim Hawkins, and I began moving toward final editing and publication.

I am grateful for the opportunity to have known Armis Hawkins, however briefly, and for his wish that I bring this beguiling work before a larger audience of readers. I appreciate the cooperation and help of Pat Hawkins, Armis Hawkins's devoted widow, and the support and friendship of Jim, who tenaciously and patiently persevered to see that his father's book was published. I am pleased to have played a part.

JoAnne Prichard Morris

Dale Hawkins Carr

Armis E. Hawkins
1920–2006

ARMIS E. HAWKINS

Country Lawyer and Friend

by Michael P. Mills

All those dead in the past never lived before our definition gives them life, and out of the shadow their eyes implore us.

—Robert Penn Warren, *All the King's Men*

Armis Eugene Hawkins was a man blessed with a tender heart and a nimble wit—an intellectual who delighted in the opera and highbrow classics; a provincial who loved the common people of our red-hilled hamlets and towns of north Mississippi. He liked to talk. He loved to laugh. And he was a good listener.

Armis and I became friends in the early 1980s when I was first elected to the state legislature and Armis had recently become a justice of the Mississippi Supreme Court. By that time, he had fought the Japanese and the Ku Klux Klan, prosecuted and defended bootleggers and drug dealers, run a statewide campaign for public office, dabbled in national politics, and won big money cases for rich and poor in the courtrooms of north Mississippi.

I came to know him well over the last twenty-five years of his life. Since Armis's home in Houston was not far from mine in Aberdeen, I occasionally gave him a ride to work in Jackson. Standing six feet four inches tall, Justice Hawkins was as slender as a blade of Johnson grass, and he had to fold himself nearly in half to squeeze into the tiny two-door Subaru I drove in those days. Once he was settled in, off we went down the Natchez Trace, and the stories began to fly. Armis was in his early sixties then—nearly four decades senior to the still-wet-behind-the-ears young lawyer driving him. But age never factored into our friendship.

Both of us loved telling and retelling anecdotes and humorous tales about our fellow Mississippians, and each found in the other an eager and appreciative listener. A master storyteller, Armis was a sensitive observer of life who found humor in the most outrageous events and virtue in the least among us. He could move from the absurd to the profound in an instant. I can see him now, his head slightly tucked to keep from bumping the ceiling, a shock of unruly hair falling onto his forehead and a boyish grin threatening to light up his face as the tale reached its resolution. I knew it was a good one when a deep, visceral rumble began just above his belt and proceeded upward, ending in a loud liberating "Ah . . . Haaaaah . . . Haaaah," with his head tilted back, the moment not to be resolved till his head swung forward again, chin touching chest, as he caught his breath.

After his passing in February 2006, I learned of *The Grand Leader* from his son Jim. But I was not surprised that Armis had spent many of his last days composing what turned out to be his first novel—or that his story brings to life the simple county people he loved.

Writing in the tradition of Mark Twain, Armis weaves his tale in the vernacular of the north Mississippi hill folk of the 1930s that he knew as a youngster.

In this "little yarn," as Armis called it, he sums up a lifetime of observing his fellow man. It is a morality play, a fable that dramatizes the eternal conflicts between truth and deception, common decency and pompous demagoguery, good and evil. The underlying themes are weighty ones, but not for a moment is *The Grand Leader* stuffy or moralistic. Armis's yarn overflows with comical characters, outlandish situations, and playful humor that would make Mr. Twain himself proud.

The Grand Leader, in fact, mocks those who pass themselves off as grand leaders. Armis had seen enough so-called "grand leaders" is his life—Bilbo, George Wallace, Jimmy Swaggart, and the list goes on—to have deep reservations about anyone, whether preacher or politician, who claims to be a savior of the people. On one of our many drives across Mississippi, Armis told me that he had seen two preachers die and that both died with fear in their eyes. I think we may meet those preachers in the fictional characters of the lazy, scripture-spouting Uncle Mayfield and the scheming, fear-mongering Brother Kato Spode. The truly admirable characters in the story are the hard-working, trusting people of the earth—the nurturing, self-sacrificing Josie, perhaps based on Armis's own beloved mother, and the narrator, Armis's alter ego, Hershell, who believes "hit's a good apple in ever barrel of rotten ones." The real grand leaders are not the ones who pass themselves off as such, but the good apples. And the good apples will save us.

The truth and humor in his little yarn are the hallmark of the well-lived public and private life of Armis Hawkins, a true grand leader.

Armis E. Hawkins

Armis Eugene Hawkins was born in Natchez on November 11, 1920, Armistice Day, commemorating the end of War I. In honor of the auspicious date of his birth, Charles Mayfield Hawkins and Lela Hill Hawkins named their second son Armis.

Mayfield and Lela both grew up in Calhoun County. Mayfield's father Hal had immigrated to the Pontotoc Ridge in the early 1800s and was present at the signing of the Chickasaw Treaty of 1832. Some of Hal's family, according to family lore, had lived earlier in the Natchez area. In 1920, Mayfield was thirty years old, a young man on the move, and Natchez on the Mississippi River was still one of the state's most urban areas, and good farmland was available on both sides of the river. Unlike the Delta, Natchez had history and remnants of high culture. Precisely when Armis's parents moved to Natchez is not known, but Mayfield registered for the WWI draft in Adams County in 1917 or 1918, but the war ended before he was called to serve.

When Armis arrived in the Hawkins household, his father owned a dry goods store in downtown Natchez, named The Grand Leader—an intriguing intimation. During the 1920s Mayfield bought and sold land and businesses and houses, for a brief time owning Stanton Hall, the crown jewel of antebellum Natchez architecture, as well a grand late nineteenth century house designed by Stanford White. He accumulated some seven thousand acres of fertile Mississippi and Louisiana farmland, including two plantations—Ivanhoe, south of Natchez, and Haphazard in Waterproof, Louisiana. Armis enjoyed childhood privileges and advantages common to well-born southerners of that era. He received an excellent grade school education. His mother,

Lela, insisted that he learn to play the violin and encouraged him to read great literature. He listened to Mozart and Beethoven on the family Victrola.

The Great Depression of the 1930s ended young Armis's genteel way of life. By 1930 his father had lost nearly everything, as a result, first, of the disastrous 1927 flood and then the national economic paralysis that followed the stock market crash in 1929. The Hawkins family spent the next few years moving from town to town—Kosciusko, Gibson, Belmont, Fulton, Flora, Memphis—as his father tried to find secure employment. They finally went to Houston, Mississippi, where Lela's brother owned a store and Lela could work. Not long afterward, however, she was diagnosed with tuberculosis and in 1936 confined in a sanatorium south of Jackson. (She stayed there off and on until her death in 1940.) His father moved to Jackson when Lela entered the sanatorium. Armis was effectively on his own at the age of sixteen.

Armis, however, refused to surrender to the mean circumstances life had handed him. He graduated from Houston High School in 1938 and then joined the New Deal's Civilian Conservation Corps. He was stationed at a work camp in Perry County in south Mississippi. Of the thirty dollars a month the CCC paid him for digging ditches and planting pine seedlings in south Mississippi, he sent twenty-five dollars back to help pay his mother's expenses and support his father.

Somehow he managed to save enough money to enter Wood Junior College, a small Methodist school in nearby Webster County. Armis soon found that Wood's mission was not entirely academic. Wood students spent a great deal of time studying the Bible and praying. Their personal behavior was strictly regulated. Cigarette smoking, for instance, was an expellable offense, and, even worse, according to Armis's code of ethics, "It was our Christian duty to 'tell on' any of our friends we saw using tobacco."

Most of the teachers at Wood were Yankee missionaries who fancied themselves called by God to civilize the poor, young southerners placed within their charge. One of the missionary ladies, assuming the freshman students didn't know how to use modern bathroom facilities, instructed them to consult the second-year students for guidance. Armis never forgot her misguided condescension. I came to know that Armis had a healthy suspicion of authority, secular and ecclesiastical, and I believe these attributes sprouted at Woods Junior College.

Armis eluded the missionaries long enough to make one thrilling discovery. One lonesome Saturday night, he wandered into the deserted central office building and turned on an old radio. As he twisted the knob, he came upon a sound he had never heard before. He was transfixed by the fast rhythms dancing from the speaker. The lyrics were familiar—"A tisket, a tasket, a green and yellow basket"—but behind the words were a thumping bass and a lively saxophone. Armis had discovered jazz! "At that moment," he told me, "my loneliness disappeared and the world made a little more sense." But not for long. The Yankee headmistress came running out and demanded that he "turn off that filthy music" and listen to "nice music" or none at all.

After only one semester at Wood, Armis borrowed money from his mother's family, the Hills, to attend Ole

Miss. Returning to campus early one December Sunday morning after a night visiting honky-tonks in Vardaman, he learned that the Japanese had bombed Pearl Harbor. The following June (1942), having finished the ROTC program at Ole Miss, he joined the United States Marines. After a few weeks of training, Armis went into combat as a private in Guadalcanal. The Marines soon recognized his natural leadership abilities and sent him to Quantico, Virginia, for officer's training. He returned to the Pacific as a First Lieutenant, and fought all the way to Tokyo.

When the war was over, Armis went back to Ole Miss and in 1947 received his law degree. Determined to "rid Mississippi of Bilboism and Prohibition," Armis opened a law practice in Houston. The following year he married Pat Burrow, an Ole Miss beauty from Clarksdale. Armis didn't wait long to give his new Delta wife a taste of what kind of life lay before her. In 1949 he joined an ill-fated effort to legalize the sale of beer in Chickasaw County.

Another supporter of legalization was a local personality I'll call "Jimbo." Jimbo was one of those characters who hang around county courthouses in Mississippi, swapping knives and gossip, hoping to pick up a little cash money by helping lawyers pick juries, foreclose on property, and carry out other worthy endeavors. True to his ilk, Jimbo enjoyed an independent mind and mood. He had no fear of expressing himself on matters of state and local import, since, like several of friends, he had a wife with a full-time job at the garment factory, who made enough to keep the family afloat.

Armis and Jimbo joined forces and went right to

work collecting the requisite signatures to call for an election. The response from the bootleggers and the churches was swift. The bootleggers immediately began clearing lots next to the school and the churches, ostensibly to open beer parlors and saloons.

In many Mississippi small towns, church members of different denominations won't even celebrate Easter Sunday together, but when some fellow files a beer petition, those same people will bond tighter than a rusty Mason fruit jar lid. In a rare display of ecumenical brotherhood, all the churches in Houston pooled their resources and paid a Texas evangelist to come in with his big tent and lead a countywide revival, where he and the local good men of the cloth railed against the evils of alcohol.

The Baptist, Methodist, and Presbyterian preachers kept up their vociferous condemnations in long-winded Sunday sermons. Even the schools got involved, with the English teachers assigning essays on "The Evils of Strong Drink." It wasn't long before many of those who had already signed the petition began sheepishly sneaking into the courthouse to remove their names. The prohibition movement peaked on election day. The high school band played "Bringing in the Sheaves" and marched behind a big white banner emblazoned in red with the words "SAVE CHICKASAW COUNTY FOR CHRIST," as they led a parade of prohibitionists through downtown Houston. The election results were never in doubt.

Jimbo and his buddies were not magnanimous losers, and they gathered outside town at a barn on Highway 15 to mourn their loss. In the manner of their ancient Druid brethren, they proceeded posthaste to get drunk on bootleg beer and moonshine whiskey. Jimbo's courage increased as the night went on. Around midnight he felt inspired to call the preachers who had organized the opposition and advise them of his feelings on the matter. He called the Baptist preacher first. When the well-trained preachers' wife answered the phone, Jimbo demanded, "Put Brother ______ on the phone." The Baptist preacher took the receiver and got an earful of Jimbo's impassioned message: "You're a lying sonofabitch and if you'll come down here on Highway 15, I'll give you a good whuppin'!" The shocked preacher hung up on him.

Next, Jimbo rang the Presbyterian elder, whose his wife also did telephone duty for her husband. The preacher took the phone, Jimbo unleashed the same profane tirade, and the offended Presbyterian hung up. Ever more emboldened, Jimbo moved on to the Methodist minister and went through the same routine. After Jimbo had finished giving his now-perfected scurrilous rant, the Methodist preacher calmly responded, "God loves you, my son." Jimbo was taken aback for a moment, but he soon recovered, and replied, "Why, God don't think no more of me and you than He does a damn swamp rabbit!"

The next day a delegation of preachers and elders and deacons descended upon the county courthouse. Jimbo was charged with three counts of public profanity. Armis, who, of course, had to defend Jimbo, demurred to the charges against his client, arguing that no crime had occurred since no federal or state law prohibited any language, profane or otherwise, on the telephone. The courtroom was packed for Armis's argument—bootleggers and preachers on one side,

Jimbo's rowdies on the other. Armis eloquently argued his motion before the judge. He was sure of success. His cause was just, his client undeniably innocent. The old circuit judge listened patiently to Armis's argument and then to the county attorney's response. When both lawyers had had their say, the Judge looked out over the packed courtroom and rendered his judgment:

> *I don't know if there is any law in this State against profaning on the telephone the good men of our community who are charged by our dear Savior with the task of preaching the Gospel. I don't know that there is any such law in this Country. In fact, I can't say that there is any such law anywhere else under the sun. But, Mr. Hawkins, there is such a law in this court. Your demurrer is over-ruled!*

Jimbo was convicted on all counts.

Armis Hawkins rapidly gained a reputation as a skillful and colorful attorney, but his practice was hardly lucrative. His clients in those years were mostly bootleggers, ne'r-do-wells, and others with few material assets, people for whom he felt a natural compassion. His family was growing: Janice was born in 1949, and by the beginning of 1951 a second child (Jean Anne) was on the way. Pat, who had provided extra income teaching school, would need to stay at home with their two children. To address these financial realities, thirty-year-old Armis borrowed money (again from the Hills) and entered the 1951 race for district attorney. "Old Enough to Know; Young Enough to Go" was his campaign slogan. Armis defeated his only opponent, Oxford's city attorney, more than two to one. Armis was unopposed for reelection in 1955 and served until 1959.

As DA, Armis launched head on into the touchiest issues, prosecuting bootleggers and closing down beer joints. He even called in federal authorities to help him locate and prosecute licensed physicians who were over-prescribing narcotics and, as he publicly proclaimed, turning many "good, otherwise law-abiding, men and women" of his district into "slaves to the narcotics habit."

His aggressive prosecution of a Benton County school superintendent for embezzlement drew crowds to the Ashland courthouse ("even those too sick to go to church" were there, according to one local wag). The spectators were rewarded for their efforts, as the Memphis *Commercial Appeal* reported:

> *Of oratory displayed during final arguments the most eloquent was Dist. Pros. Att. Armis Eugene Hawkins.*
>
> *The thirty-five-year-old prosecutor, who towers more than six feet, had to reach low to pound the counsel table. He frequently dabbed a handkerchief at his eyes while quoting scripture or charging that [the defendant] sent the people's money "flowing down Corruption Creek."*

The guilty verdict shocked prognosticators and made news throughout Mississippi and in nearby states.

Armis Hawkins, the crusading district attorney who was cleaning up government in north Mississippi, was making a name for himself throughout the state. He was a life-long friend and ally of J. P. Coleman, (governor of Mississippi, 1956–1960, and justice and chief justice of the U.S. Fifth Circuit Court of Appeals, 1965–1983. During Armis's first term as DA, Coleman was attorney general for the state and often called upon Armis to prosecute sensitive cases outside Armis' home district. Citizens committees and prosecutors in Natchez and other areas demanded his counsel.

Those years were a time of racial unrest and Ku

Klux Klan violence. Armis's sense of fairness and dedication to the law and humanity sometimes put him in danger. One such occasion involved a Klansman charged with committing a hate crime. At the time, Armis drove a 1955 Chrysler New Yorker with a powerful V-8 engine. It had no air-conditioner, so Armis placed white sheets on the mohair seats to reflect the hot summer sun. The jury finally returned a verdict late in the evening. As the involved parties were leaving the courthouse, Armis noticed a couple of pick-up trucks trailing him. When he turned onto the highway, they turned too. When he sped up, so did the pick-ups. As the trucks came closer, Armis saw that the drivers and their passengers were dressed in all white. The Klan! Shots were fired. And the pickups kept coming.

Armis gunned his big Hemi engine, and the Chrysler roared on, with his own white sheets flapping and billowing out the open windows as the big machine topped a hundred miles per hour. Armis kept his eyes on the rear view mirror: "Objects may be closer than they appear!" He wasn't taking any chances. The speedometer needle was as far to the right as it would go, and the sheets were still flapping. On one long stretch of highway, Armis watched as the pick-ups became smaller and smaller and their lights were tiny pinpoints. But he kept that big engine at top speed until the "Entering Chickasaw County" sign came into view. He was home. He had outrun the Klan.

When his second term as district attorney ended, Armis was ready to expand his horizons. Well known in political circles throughout the state and encouraged by people in his district, he became a candidate for lieutenant governor. He campaigned as a progressive in a mean era of racial pandering. Only five years after the Brown decision ordering desegregation of the schools, Mississippi was in a frenzy of resistance, led by the Citizens Council and supported by the state's Sovereignty Commission. There were fewer than 20,000 registered black voters in the state, and no candidate for state office could get elected by declaring himself for integration. Armis explained his approach in a speech delivered in Greenwood, titled "A Call to Sanity."

> *If I am examined and the physician finds symptoms of cancer, I hope to be cured by knowledge and experience. I do not propose to turn to voodoo. The same approach should prevail as regards our racial situation. Yet there are those who think that by loud noises, waving of arms and stomping of feet, our public officials and leaders can drive the evil sprit of integration away. Political quackery is just as imbecilic as medicinal quackery . . . Only intelligence and straight thinking can save us.*

Unfortunately, Mississippi wasn't ready for straight thinking. Armis lost to Paul B. Johnson, Jr., who had already run unsuccessfully for governor three times and would later "Stand Tall" against integration at Ole Miss. Ross Barnett was elected governor. It's difficult to imagine Armis Hawkins as Ross Barnett's lieutenant governor, but what a difference his voice of sanity and an ounce of his courage might have made.

Following this loss, Armis accepted his friend U. S. Senator James O. Eastland's appeal to run the Democratic Party's statewide presidential campaign for John F. Kennedy in 1960. Armis promptly took the offense against the two opposing groups—the "unpledged" Democrats (those who didn't support the national party) led by Governor Barnett, and Wirt Yerger, Jr.'s growing band of state Republicans, who supported

Richard Nixon. Surprising local political observers who had questioned whether "loyalist" Democrats could wage a strong race for Kennedy, Armis put together an impressive campaign organization and set a feverish pace of public speaking. He never missed an opportunity to challenge the unpledged group for their "hopeless proposals" or "vile and vicious statement." Without hesitation, Armis lashed out at the Republicans for "sugarcoating their platform" and declared that Nixon" cares no more about Mississippi than he does for a swamp rat."

Armis organized scores of successful events throughout the state, involving his friends, Senators Stennis and Eastland, former governor Coleman, U.S. Congressman Jamie Whitten, along with numerous other state office holders and a string of U.S. Senators from other southern states. He also brought in former president Harry Truman to stump for Kennedy; ten thousand cheering people came out to hear Truman at the Tupelo fairgrounds.

When the votes were counted, Armis had managed to bring John Kennedy within two and one-half percentage points of winning Mississippi, the state that only a year before had elected rabble-rousing, race-baiting Ross Barnett governor. Out of nearly 300,000 votes cast statewide, Barnett's "unpledged" electors won by fewer than 7,800 votes. Nixon came in a distant third, though he had personally campaigned in the state.

After the two-year flurry of political campaigning, recognizing that a future in elective state politics was not promising for a progressive or moderate, Armis returned to the full-time practice of law in Houston in

1961. Now the father of three children—Janice, Jean Anne, and a son, Jim, born in 1954—he devoted himself to building a successful country law practice, improving his community, and enjoying his family.

Country lawyers belong to a dying breed in our modern era of specialization, and Armis Hawkins was the epitome of the breed. In those days trial lawyers actually tried cases. A good country lawyer represented a board or two, defended a few criminals for a modest fee, represented plaintiffs when the case was promising, and counseled civil defendants when the opportunities presented themselves. Armis spent the 1960s and '70s representing rich and poor with equal vigor, defending some of the same people he had prosecuted as DA. He also served as attorney for the county board of supervisors, which kept him in touch with his old political connections. Even so, his connections didn't always predict success. One of his biggest political embarrassments was that his friend William Winter lost Chickasaw County to Evelyn Gandy in the 1979 governor's race.

With his tailored suits, trademark suspenders, and size 14 AAA Allen Edmonds shoes, Armis was quite a presence in the county courthouses of north Mississippi. From 1960 to 1980, he matched wits with some of the best trial lawyers in the South and, according to son Jim, never lost a single trial case. Nationally recognized as one of the nation's top attorneys, Armis remained ever the country lawyer.

Armis's gentlemanly demeanor belied a certain roguishness within, and his "inner rogue" found its way out from time to time. Quick to apply rules to others, Armis sometimes lapsed when applying them to himself. Occasionally it was the fate of a young, green lawyer to go up against the seasoned pro, and such was the situation when Claude Clayton, Jr., opposed Armis in the last jury case Armis tried before going on the state Supreme Court. The trial took place in Armis's home county before Circuit Judge W. W. Brown. Armis had sued Clayton's client, a trucking company, for damages caused when one of its trucks, pulling a load of logs, crossed over a double yellow line and collided head-on with the plaintiff's car. The liability was not in dispute; the only real issue was how much money the trucking firm would have to pay the plaintiff, represented by Armis.

Armis called the plaintiff—a petite young lady—to the stand. Then he unhurriedly removed his tailored coat, carefully laid it across the back of his chair, and ignoring the podium altogether, strolled over to the jury box. Hooking his thumbs in his red suspenders, he began leading the young lady through the many horrors of her accident and guiding her in a gripping account of her injuries in all their excruciating detail.

Although Claude could see that the jury was deeply moved by her testimony, he politely made no objection to the leading questions his distinguished elder continually asked. When Armis finished his direct examination, he turned toward Claude and, as though doing the young lawyer a favor, he said, "You may want to ask Miss ______ a few questions." Claude quickly glanced up to see if Judge Brown would respond to the invasion of the Court's authority by the plaintiff's counsel, but the judge just sat there impassively.

Gathering his notes, Claude went directly to the podium and began his cross-examination. He was well prepared. After asking only a few introductory questions, Claude noticed that the jurors were distracted by something, but he continued with his examination. Soon, however, the loud mumbling in the courtroom made his concentration impossible. He looked across the room and saw what the jurors saw: Armis engaged in a spirited conversation with the circuit clerk, completely ignoring Claude's cross-examination. The judge still said nothing, and Claude struggled on. Eventually Armis took his seat.

As the young lawyer finally got to his most important questions, he realized that the jurors had again shifted their attention, this time to something behind him. Claude stopped his examination and turned all the way around to see what was distracting the jurors this time. Now, Armis was carrying on a chuckling conversation with a group of lawyers who had just entered the room. Armis was obviously indifferent to the questions Claude wanted to ask the plaintiff, and, even worse, the jurors were, too!

Claude felt he had no option but to object to the senior attorney's courtroom behavior: "Your Honor, I hate to raise an objection, but I must object to Mr. Hawkins walking around the courtroom and talking to the clerk and visiting other lawyers while I am trying to cross-examine the plaintiff. Can you please instruct Mr. Hawkins to remain in his seat while I am examining witnesses?"

"Mr. Clayton," the judge replied. "I've been trying to get him to stop doing that for fifteen years. What makes you think he's going to change now?"

Armis became not only a successful, prosperous attorney; he was one of the last of the fine men and women who believed a lawyer should serve his community. During his years in Houston, he became active in economic development and worked tirelessly to bring new industries to Chickasaw County. For a time in the late fifties and sixties, the small town of Houston offered more industrial jobs than Tupelo.

Armis avidly supported the local industries and the hospital, as his contribution to bettering the lives of his fellow citizens in that poor area of the state. The local people returned the favor. Many who had struggled trying to make a living farming were able to get good jobs, and some of them later chose Armis as their attorney. Armis also represented several of the industries in both local and federal matters.

In 1980 Armis was elected to the Mississippi Supreme Court, and he served until 1995 as justice, presiding justice, and chief justice. Demonstrating courage, keen intellect, and engaging wit, he distinguished himself as a principled, independent jurist. As Sid Salter, editorial writer for the Jackson *Clarion-Ledger* wrote, Chief Justice Hawkins was one of those "public officials who hold the public trust in their hands as if it were the most fragile piece of crystal—bright and shining and easily broken if mishandled." He was known among his colleagues as a legal scholar, a prolific writer, and a dynamic leader.

Armis's leadership led directly to the landmark 1992 decision in which the Mississippi Supreme Court decided (5–4) that the state could retry self-described white supremacist Byron De La Beckwith for the 1963 murder of civil rights leader Medgar Evers. Beckwith had been tried for the murder twice by all-white juries in the 1960s. Although both trials had ended in hung juries, the matter of a new trial after thirty years raised such constitutional issues as the defendant's right to a speedy trial and due process. Armis wrote the majority opinion, explaining in plain, simple terms that "Society . . . has the right to a criminal justice system that is not a toothless tiger." The controversial decision led to a new trial and Beckwith's conviction and life sentence in 1994 (upheld by Miss. S.C. in 1997), generating widespread national attention and inspiring several books and a major motion picture. Since then, several Mississippi civil rights murder cases of the 1960s, which had never been prosecuted, have been reopened and brought to trial.

In a case concerning a legislator's conflict of interest, the defendant had argued that the language prohibiting self-dealing by government officials was too broad and imprecise to apply. Armis dismissed the defendant's argument with characteristic clarity and spunk: "We are not called upon to define the edge of a target in a case where the defendant has scored a bull's eye."

During his tenure as chief justice, Armis guided the court through a vital reform of the judicial system. To improve the state's ability to handle cases and provide Mississippians with more access, he spearheaded the creation of a court of appeals and the Administrative Office of Courts. Armis also spoke out vehemently against the large amounts of money judges raised to get elected as guaranteeing the corruption of our court system. "Absolute impartiality is the keystone to justice," he said. "A judge who cannot be impartial is nothing." In a prophetic speech to the Mississippi legislature in 1995, Armis implored the lawmakers to "keep the money changers out of our Mississippi temples of justice."

Chief Justice Hawkins retired from the Court in 1995 and went home to Houston to practice law. No longer constrained by the vagaries of making a living, he began to write extensively and take on causes that he felt strongly about. Having been an active member of the Mississippi Bar Association's ethics committee, he was instrumental in creating the "Professionalism Handbook" and the Mississippi Rules of Professional Conduct. He represented indigent citizens against corporations who took advantage of them. He took on the state's criminal justice system for its over-reaching tactics. He wrote legal opinions and analyses for other attorneys, as he was frequently asked to do. Indeed he never stopped making his opinions known—whether on weighty Constitutional issues or purely political ones. He particularly enjoyed writing letters to the editor.

In 2003 during the gubernatorial campaign between Republican Haley Barbour and Democrat Ronnie Musgrove, Armis wrote the Jackson *Clarion Ledger* about Barbour's statement that "children attending Head Start lived (in an environment) so bad they would be better off sitting up on a piano bench in a whorehouse." Feisty as ever, Armis needled the Republican candidate with obvious delight, as this excerpt shows. (He intentionally misspelled Barbour's name—or, as he explained in a postscript—"corrected" it.)

> *I am sure that not one man or woman in 100,000 in Mississippi has the faintest firsthand knowledge of the inside of a whorehouse. Except for this infinitesimal few of our State's inhabitants, the inside of a whorehouse, especially one with piano, is*

as unfamiliar as the far side of the moon. Unless one has been inside a whorehouse during business hours, one cannot possibly know its environment. Indeed, the statement is meaningless—it can mean anything the listener chooses to imagine.

The literature I have read treats whorehouses rather kindly, it seems to me.—e.g., Rhett Butler lived part of the time in a whorehouse and it didn't seem to bother Scarlett too much. Indeed, the lady proprietress of that enterprise (I forget her name) was something of a hero when Sherman put the torch to Atlanta. And in life, Scott Joplin and W.C. Handy each performed during their formative years as musicians in whorehouses. It seems to me one could end his life worse off than having composed, respectively, "Maple Leaf Rag" or "St. Louis Blues," classics still popular a century after their composition. . . .

Unlike the overwhelming majority of Mississippians, however, Mr. Barber (sic) clearly knew what he meant. . . . He is a candidate for our state's highest office and would not dare make a statement about which he is totally ignorant. Perhaps Mr. Barber will enlighten us on his first hand knowledge of what goes on inside a whorehouse, especially one with a piano. . . .

During his last few years, Armis was the senior member of a book club, consisting of Ole Miss Chancellor Robert Khayat, Itawamba Community College President David Cole, Dr. Andy Mullins, and myself. The five of us would occasionally gather and discuss a work of literature. The Chancellor named us the "Particles," after the theme of a book we once discussed, *God's Debris*, by Scott Adams. Armis was our main "particle." He never failed to read the assignment, never missed a meeting, and never lost patience with our sometimes-clumsy efforts to grasp the truth. Armis delighted in responding in writing to our views and arguments. I always looked forward to his letters commenting on literature and life. I was saddened when he wrote the

Particles in 2005 to say he would no longer be able to able to meet with us. He had begun preparing for the end.

The last book he suggested that our group read was Robert Penn Warren's classic novel, *All the King's Men,* about the compelling and corrupting power of politics. Unfortunately, Armis died before we had an opportunity to discuss it with him. In this magnificent book, the narrator finally understands what Armis must have perceived many years before—that each of us bears responsibility for the consequences of our actions, that we all face the burden of our history, that we go "into the convulsion of the world, out of history into history and the awful responsibility of Time."

Armis Eugene Hawkins departed the convulsion of the world on February 28, 2006. We are fortunate that, among his many legacies, he left us this yarn—his own droll insights into corruption and responsibility. Set squarely among the people of the north Mississippi hills, *The Grand Leader* is a both a tribute to his past and a cheering evocation of the man who wrote it.

The Grand Leader

PROLOGUE

I don't reckon you ever heard tell of a coral snake, much less seen one.

Well, they little old snakes about twict as long as a nickel pencil, a little bit bigger around than one of them two-bit bamboo fishing pole canes like they sell at Gozer's Hardware, with black and kinda orange-red and yellow circles around 'em.

Fact is, they ain't too much bigger'n a worm, and you might even say kinda cute. And, if you was to just be, say, chopping cotton and uncover one, and you wasn't, just say, petrified of *any* snake, why you might be as likely to pick him up and look at him as you would be to chop him in two with your hoe.

I never would advise you to pick him up, though, 'cause one of them coral snakes has more pizen in its belly than any ten diamondback rattlers or any fifteen cottonmouths. And, if he was to bite you, well, as Dave Kyle says, "That would be the end of the deal." Your deal, that is. Twenty-three skidoo, kid!

Still, something else about them coral snakes. If you was to happen to pick one up and that's all you done, he probly would just try and wriggle away. And, if you was either careless, or had sense enough to let him have his way, he probly, just probly, would wriggle loose from you and leave you as fast as a snake can. (They ain't no rattler nor moccasin; you might say they timid, shy.) And you never would be no wiser or know how near you just come to your Maker.

If coral snakes wasn't thataway, they shorely would be a lot more dead folks down at the butt end of the Mississippi River and the Gulf Coast where the land is swampy, and it is wetter and hotter, which is where them snakes mostly are. I was just like you probly are, knowed nothing about no coral snake, never seen one, never heard tell of one (and don't care to see nair 'nother one now). We live in the Flatwoods country about 150 mile north of the Gulf Coast, and them little monsters just ain't in this country. Leastwise, nobody I ever knowed, knowed anything about them.

I found out all I have told you after all the terrible things what happened to my uncle Mayfield—by marriage—Yancy. After the funeral I got so curious—things just didn't fit—that I taken it on myself to go to that place where they got books on everything, the Carnegie library at the county seat. First trip.

Hit's a red brick building. Inside they's oak hardwood floors so shiny you can see yourself in 'em, and the smell of polish hits you when you first open the door. They got signs everwheres saying, "Quiet!" "Quiet!," which don't make too much sense with them floors, 'cause you make a racket ever step you take unless you get on your tiptoes, which I done when I seen the signs. And, lordamercy, the books. Everwheres. Musta been four or five hundred on all them shelves.

Anyway, a kindly white-headed lady come up and asked me, "May I help you?"

When I told her, lady, I need to know something about snakes, she went and got a real thick book called HERPATOLOGY, which had pictures and told about snakes all over. Sure enough, in there was all about coral snakes, including about where they was most likely to be.

So now I can tell you the whole story, without no gaps.

ONE

This whole trouble started this year—19 and 38—back in the spring, when that uncle of mine—by marriage—Mayfield Yancy, taken it upon hisself to make a preacher. And got hisself all tangled up with Kato Spode.

Why'd he decide to be a preacher? Why would *anybody* want to be a preacher? Your guess is good as mine. I don't know what's in their head. Except I will say if anybody was going to make a preacher, he was a good candidate. Religion was his one long suit. Fact is, his only one (unless you add on getting out of work).

Uncle May always was what most folks would call "different." I'm a Mooneyham, though, and not bragging, but none us Mooneyhams ever been accused of being short on horse sense, except maybe my aunt

Josie for marrying him. When Grandma passed away, Aunt Josie moved in and was living with us.

Them two met at Morgan & Lindsey's store. Hit's on the west side of the court square in the county seat. Don't know what taken her there, but she always said he was looking for needles and some thread to patch up his Sunday britches. He asked her what he oughta get.

That night around the supper table, Josie was all grins. "You ain't goner believe this, Gertrude."

"What's this here I ain't goner believe?"

"This man I met today. He had on a pair of high yaller patent leather low quarters, Gertrude. They was cracked, squeaked ever step he taken, and square's a box in front. Them shoes had to be at least ten year old. And a green sock on one foot and a white un on t'other! His britches and shirt both need needles and thread and patches aplenty."

"Um-m-m, hum."

"But he had on a necktie."

"'Pears like you give him a lot of lookin' over, Josie," Mama laughed.

"Whatever else he is, or he ain't, Gertrude," Josie told her, "he ain't no bum."

Marrying him was the one dumb thing I ever knowed her to do. But ain't that something else you never know, why a woman marries some guy? She wasn't the prettiest woman in the county, and she had got to be almost twenty-two.

Still . . .

He taken her to that 121 acres of his at Halls Siding out in the Flatwoods.

Us Mooneyhams are Pontotoc ridge folks, been there since before the Civil War with them Yankees. Pontotoc ridge land is red, with clay and loam mixed just right, on lowback hills, well drained, and can always be counted on to make a fair to middling crop, year in and out. It ain't rich as Skuner bottom or some of that Delta, but you ain't gonna get flooded neither, or et up with boll weevils. You might not hit no home run making a crop on Pontotoc ridge, but you ain't never gonna strike out, neither.

Them Flatwoods is something else. Gray as a corpse, dirt there ain't never just right. When crops getting too much rain, Flatwoods land gets wetter'n anywheres else, and when they ain't getting enough rain, Flatwoods land is dryer'n anywheres else. Water sets for days after hit's done rained, and in dry spells the ground cracks open like a plate you dropped. Mules do plenty of sweating pulling a plow through gummy Flatwoods dirt. Whatever the ground is anywheres else hit's worse in them Flatwoods. Many's the time I've heard my paw say that old Flatwoods land is so poor even the federal land bank wouldn't make no loan on it.

I always heard that sixty, seventy year ago—hit was after the war—the Flatwoods was covered in white oak timber. Stands fifty foot or more high. No finer timber nowhere, not the whole world. Then along about then, Yankee Jews come down and bought up all the land, set up sawmills and planing mills and begun cleaning out the timber. White oak lumber made everthing from barrels for Tennessee whisky and French wine to furniture for kings and queens. They won some kind of world prize, so I heard. The M&O and the GM&N built the two railroads we got running through the county to carry the lumber north. (They tell me now this year, 19 and 38, they about to close the M&O branch line and sell it all for scrap iron to Japan.)

Not just them Yankees, but some county men, too, got well off Flatwoods timber. Built them big houses you can see over at the county seat, and started banks. Mr. Dabney Biffle, the First State Bank's owner, and Mr. Jessie Armstead, at Farmers and Merchants—both their paps started out timber and peckerwood sawmill men before they taken hit on theyselves to be bankers. So I always heard.

Anyways, finally, after thirty or forty years, the timber was all cleaned out. No more white oak. All that cutover land sold for two bits to four bits an acre. Uncle May's old man—a sawmill roustabout hisself—had bought this 121-acre spot for fifty dollars out there at Halls Siding, and give hit to him before he taken off for parts unknown. And that's where Uncle May taken Aunt Josie when they got married. Halls Siding is where the M&O branch line trains used to stop in the old days to load on timber. Train didn't stop there no more (unless hit was flagged down).

My folks, Paw (her brother), had saw enough of Uncle May to figure him and her wasn't going to make hit by theyselves. And he sure enough knowed hit when he drove over to Uncle May's and taken a look. "He ain't got no more'n maybe five or six acres cleared," Paw said. "They's scrub oaks and some hickry scattered over the place ain't good for nothin' but firewood. They mixed in with stumps, bresh and vines, blackgum and sweetgum saplins all tangled togather so thick you have to kick ever step walkin' through it. And slews."

"What about the house?" Mama asked.

"Three rooms, pine siding outside wall, with a curled-up tin roof rustin' out."

"How about they kitchen?"

"Cookstove Mayfield said come from a scrap-iron pile over at the ice plant. They got lard bucket lids for plates, and drinkin' out of fruit jars." Then he said, "And they ain't even got a necessary house."

So they decided to send me to stay with them. Not before Paw give me a talking, though. We'd slopped the hogs, fed the stock, and just milked. Sun was setting, and we was out in the barn lot starting back to the house.

He stopped, rolled and lit hisself a cigarette. "You know about farmin', Hershell. I've saw to that. You goner need all I've larnt you where you headed."

"Yessir."

"They's somethin' else . . ."

"Yessir?"

"You young, little bit fiesty at times. And I've saw times when your tongue was a mite long. You come by that honest, your mama's side. Ain't many of them Stovalls what ain't got clappers for tongues."

"Yessir."

"You ain't never lived in them Flatwoods. You don't know them folks what live there. They differnt. You better remember what I'm tellin' you now."

He made sure I was listening, but I was already all ears. Ain't never been nobody smarter'n my paw.

"What's so with most folks is 'specially so with a Flatwoodser. They got hair-trigger feelins. Don't say nothin' to one of 'em what's liable—or stands a smidgen of a chanct—to git it in his head you 'puttin' him down,' or think you're thinkin' you're a bit better'n him."

"Yessir, Paw."

"They don't forgit. You could say somethin'—and he might not say nothin'—and you have no idear you done hurt his feelins. You forgit all about hit. He don't, though. Somethin' gits in a Flatwoodser's craw, hit stays there. Ten or fifteen years later he's liable to run into you somers when he's had some snorts and half geed up, and out the clear blue pull out his knife, tell you he don't 'preciate 'what you said to me that time,' and proceed to cut your guts out. They's at least one killin' ever year in them Flatwoods."

"I'll be careful, Paw."

And then he said, "A Flatwoodser'll steal 'fore he'll beg." Paw's forehead wrinkled uneasy. "They's some of 'em meaner'n blue-eyed hell."

TWO

Hit was a cold January day. Mama'd wrapped dishes, cups, forks, knives, and spoons in a box for me to take. Paw'd rigged up a wagon three sideboards high, loaded it with hoes, shovels, kizer blade, crosscut saw, axes, middle buster and turning plows, and I throwed on my old locker with all my duds in it. He harnessed up Jellie and Bean, two matched mules he'd raised, his favorites. He set on a sack of seed corn, and I taken two bushels of unshucked corn to the wagon. "Better thow in six or eight bales of hay, son. He ain't apt to have no stock feed, neither."

"Jellie's goner be a bit frisky for a ways, but she'll settle down. They's a waterin' trough there, and you kin water the team at the mule lot on the south side of the square. And headin' outta the county seat you'll cross the GM&N tracks and when you see 'Jim's Garrage' you'll know you on the right road. About six mile outta town Josie's and Mayfield's house will be on the right. On one end the roof's way yonder higher'n t'other, and just acrost the road on the left is a big ole tree, a chinerberry. When you see them, you'll know you there. Cain't miss it."

He give me a two-dollar bill. "This orter keep you in tobakker for a while." Then, "Look out after Josie," was the last thing he said.

I climbed up on the wagon seat, and tapped Bean with the reins. "Giddap!" I was a lot younger then, all full of vinegar, looking forward to getting to do something different, but when I turned around to wave Paw goodby, I seen a look made me wonder what all he was thinking.

Then I headed out the fourteen mile to Uncle Mayfield's.

Sky was gray, nobody moving out the houses. One or two stray cows or stock would be huddled together aside the bobwire fences in the pastures. Just standing there like statues. Every now and then a car'd pass by, knocking up gravel.

Sun was about half hour from sundown when I finished up watering the mules. A block west of the square there was a cafe selling "Hamburgers 5c." When I smelled 'em frying, my belly got to growling. I was about to get myself one, but I knowed Josie'd have me a good hot supper and I could save that nickel. Out at the edge of town, like Paw told me, I seen JIM'S GARRAGE. "WE FIX EVER THING. FROM FLIVVERS WHAT SHIVVERS TO STUDIEBAKES WHAT AKES. DONT MATTER."

Right next door to Jim's was a one-room shed with smoke drifting out from hit what set my belly to growling again when I got up close. Had a sign, "BAR-B-Q. BEST IN THE WORLD! SANWICHES." I'd never heard tell of BAR-B-QS, but they shore made me ready for supper. I wondered what Josie was gonna have.

A mile or so out of town was a house close by the road. Lamplight was coming out the windows. Just as I passed, out marched a man in overalls, one gallus loose and flapping, with a razor strop in one hand and aholt of a kid with t'other.

"Don't whup me, Papa. Please! Ain't gon do hit no more. Swear 'fo God I ain't'! 'Fo God, Papa."

"Naw. I know you ain't, 'cause I'm fixin' to larn you. I done told you, and I done told you *and told you*, but dammit, boy, you just wouldn't take tolding!" I wondered what that boy'd did.

Riding there, the only sound was the wagon wheels crunching the gravel, I wished I knowed how to play a French or even a "Juice" harp.

Had time for all kind of thoughts. Come to mind about being a Mooneyham. But telling hit like hit really is, they's Mooneyhams and they's Mooneyhams.

My great-grandpap Asop and great-grandmaw Perline Mooneyham begun a family just after the war in the 18 and 60s or 70s, had a bunch of children—nine all told, seems like. There was a Jew peddler them days what come in late spring and early fall, twice a year, and always spent the night at their house. He was welcome, what all he was selling, and children shore enough looked forward to seeing him come. He knowed each of their names, and they knowed he was going to have a present for every one of them, all wrapped up.

My grandpa "Issy" Mooneyham—his real name was Isadoor—was the third kid. Wasn't another with that name in the county. Still ain't, far as I know.

Well, sir, everbody seen that from a chap Issy stood out. He was darker complected and just plain brighter and smarter'n any the other kids. As a man, he outfigured and outfarmed any of his kin or neighbors, "lived by his wits" as they used to say. He had more and better farm land to leave his children than most any farmer on Pontotoc ridge. Don't think he much liked that name they give him, and till the day he died, if you wanted to get in the damndest fight in your life, just call him "Sissy Issy." Might be a lot of things said about Issy's kids, but none of 'em ever been accused of being short on brains.

Hit was graveyard talk to begin. But a long time later hit got more open, leastwise among Issy's family. Even heard that great-grandma Perline—she lived ten year or more after great-grandpap Asop passed—made some strong hints to Issy before she died. And, fact is, Issy's children become kind of proud of what they'd heard. (They was all black-headed and darker complected than their cousins, too.) Mama used to laugh. "Give 'em a pedigree," she'd say. And here I done said more than I meant to.

Hit was getting cold setting there in that wagon.

Course I never knowed her, but that Perline must of been a stepper. Uncle Zeb remembered her. "She had them dartin' kind of eyes—you could see mischief in 'em when she was ever bit of eighty." And he'd always heard in her days she *could* cut a frolic.

He said, "Onct they was having a big dance at the old man's house, neighbors from all around had come. Front parlor all cleared out, them what wasn't dancin' settin' in chairs around the wall. Two fiddlers goin' at it. 'Turkey in the Straw,' 'Buffalo Gals,' a-tearin' them fiddles up. 'Promenade,' 'Round the Round,' the caller'd call one step, then t'other.

"Hit was a cold December night around about Christmas," Uncle Zeb went on. "The boys had they-selves a jug at the woodpile outside, ever now and then, why, one would step outside and git hisself a taste. Hit was bad cold.

"One them boys had been outside and taken hisself a purty good swig and come back in. The fireplace was a-cracklin', them oak logs a-blazin'. And when he come back in, the old boy backed hisself up to the fireplace, and was standin' there to git hisself warm.

"Dancers was havin' at hit, the 'Miss Betsy' step. The gals kickin' them heels, doin' some high steppin'. Could hear they starched dresses a-whishin', the floor goin' up and down, up and down. The heat from that fire and the likker bound to have hit that boy, 'cause all at onct out he yelled, 'I SMELL P———Y!'

"Grandpaw got out the chair where he was settin'. That keg-eye of his'n what he'd got in the war—which it never done lessen he was shore enough mad—went to twitchin'.

"'I'm goin' to git my shotgun.'

"Grandmaw retched up and taken his arm. 'Wait, Paw. Wait. Kelm down. Maybe he do.'"

I got to thinking about the farm Uncle Mayfield and me working together was gonna make out of his place. We'd hit them clods first thing tomorrow, after I'd got me a good night's sleep. Him and me gonna make a "showplace," sure enough.

I wondered what Josie'd have fixed for supper. Knowed hit bound to be something good.

Hit was two hours after dark—no moon, just starlight. Still didn't have no trouble seeing a black shape of a rooftop over on my right, one end two or three foot higher'n the other, and bowed up in the middle. Over on my left across the road was that big old tree. My feet was froze, my butt was sore as a risin', and I was hungry enough to eat whit-leather. When I turned in, Josie opened a door.

"Hershell! We done give you out!"

"Boy, am I glad to git here!"

"I'll be right out."

She come out hunkered over and shivering, with just a jumper on over her nightgown, and holding a lamp. I followed her out to a shed.

"They's two stalls in here."

I seen both had a trough, went and took ten ear of corn from out the wagon and put five in each one. Then I taken the harness off Jellie and Bean, and led them in their stalls. We went back in the house.

"Have you et?"

I told her no. "Oh lordamercy! The fire done died out in the stove!" She taken a couple of cold biscuits out the stove oven. Them and molasses was my supper.

She lit another lamp and taken me to a room across a hallway. "Hershell, I'm mighty sorry. We ain't fixed up just yet for you. You goner have to sleep on a pallet."

Wasn't hardly no padding between me and the floor. A ragged quilt the only cover. I fretted, "Whyn't Mama think to send bedding with all the other stuff?" Air whistled through the outside wall. I'd shiver and shake till I'd finally get to sleep, and then wake up shaking.

Slits of daylight coming between the wall boards woke me. Getting up, I heard my bones crack. Looked around. Fireplace cold and empty. Spiderwebs in ever corner, and cardboard was stuffed in busted-out windowpanes. That pallet, my locker, a wood box, and two straight chairs with busted-out bottoms was all they was in the room. Seen my shoe tracks real plain in the floor dust.

I smelled side-meat frying and headed to the kitchen. "You still like your eggs scrambled, or want 'em fried?" "Fried, over easy, Josie." Then she brung me around with a cup of hot black coffee. I seen it didn't have no handle and remembered: "Josie, Mama sent some dishes. They out in the wagon."

"Oh, I'm so glad!"

She already had hot biscuits, sawmill gravy, and a streak of lean side meat on the table, and fried me three eggs to go with 'em. Just like Paw'd said, my plate was a Swift lard bucket lid.

I had began to feel better when Uncle Mayfield come in. I hadn't saw him the night before; he'd done gone to bed. Josie said he liked to get his sleep.

I taken my first good look at the man I was expecting for him and me together to make the best little farm in the county. Us swinging kizer blades, a hoe apiece chopping cotton, or him behind one plow and me the other in a field of new corn.

I'd say he was maybe a bit shy of five foot ten, had one of them long narrow heads shaped like a soap goard, and kinda wall-eyed. A turkey gobbler neck, and a thatch of sandy hair down over his ears. He hadn't been to no barber lately. Looked to me to be maybe eight or ten year older'n Josie.

"Uncle Mayfield, I'm here to help you with the crop."

"We glad to have you, Hershell."

"How many acres cleared?"

"Don't know, Hershell."

"About six," Josie said.

"What you aim to plant on them six acres?"

"Ain't thought too much about that, Hershell."

I et and went out on the back porch. They was a screen door but no screen atall on the top half of it. I was wondering what use that door had with just the bottom half having a screen, and not looking like I should of been when I stepped out. I fell sprawling. Back stoop didn't have no top step!

I got up offen the ground smarting and cussing, dusted myself off, seen I'd busted the bark off my shin. Then I taken a look around. The planks on the barn shed was tore loose and some missing. Half hits roof had done blowed away.

I walked around to take a look at the house. Been a long time since hit'd seen a paintbrush, if ever. Papa had told me about hit leaning, and hit shore was. What done it was rotted-out and falling-in sleepers at one end. Just a matter of time—and hit wasn't gonna be long—afore that house was gonna break or fall in.

The sky was dirty gray. Out back of the shed, and beyond what little was open land, in ever direction was a solid wall of brush and vines mixed in with saplings nothing but a rabbit could git through.

Up next to the house I seen a couple of dominicker hens squatted in loose gray dirt, not moving, and a rooster pecking at something. None hadn't bothered to scatter when I fell out the back door. Laying about in knee-high dead jimson weeds was pieces of machinery I didn't know what of, angle irons, a motor head, pistons, a busted steam boiler full of holes, all junk. Them and the tin roofs was red from rust.

Right off I knowed the few acres of land what was cleared needed busting up for cotton, corn, or a crop of some kind, if they planned to eat. I heard Josie inside: "Go on out there and give Hershell a hand, Mayfield," and he come on out.

We went out to that shed you'd call their barn, and I went to harnessing Jellie, thinking he'd go on and harness Bean. But he didn't, 'cause when I had done got through all he'd did was put a bridle on him and was just standing there.

"Uncle Mayfield, we need to harness both mules."

He started off, but dad-blamed if he didn't start to put the hames on before putting on the collar! Even Bean knowed better, 'cause he give a little buck.

"Uncle Mayfield, when I'm harnessin' the first thing I do after breshin' or curryin' the mule is to put his collar on." I showed him how to buckle on the collar.

"Then next, I put on these hames." I fitted the hames twixt the collar grooves and tied and buckled them on. "See?"

He give a couple of nods.

"Now next, you latch on these here trace chains."

And on I went, showing him how the chains hooked onto the hames and a plow. And then tied the plow lines onto the harness rings.

While I could tell plain he didn't know a dad-blamed thing about harnessing no mule, I didn't think the thing to do was to say so flat out. "Uncle Mayfield, you ain't had all that much practice harnessin', have you?"

"That's right, Hershell."

Now I knowed that if he didn't know nothing about harnessing a mule, for danged sure he wasn't gonna know the first thing about plowing. But I asked him, anyways, "How about plowin'?"

"About the same."

It begun to soak in my head then I might be in trouble. Big time.

"Uncle Mayfield, they ain't no way to farm without mules. And they's things you gotta know ef you gonna work 'em. Any mule got twict the sense of air horse that ever walked. First off, a mule got to trust you. Got to trust you. That you gon see he got plenty to eat, that he got plenty of water, good water. That even you ain't gon eat till he's done et."

"Sorta like a Good Shepherd?"

"Uh? Well—yeah, guess you might say that. But that ain't all there is you need to know about a mule. A mule has got to respect you, too. He got to know you know what you doin'. 'Cause ef you don't, he's shore goner know hit—you ain't goner fool that mule—and one them days when you ain't watchin', he'll kick the livin' hell out of you. Ain't a Mooneyham by name don't know this. And you better know hit too ef you aim to do any kind of farmin'."

That set him off. "Mules of aintchen lineage, Hershell."

"They what?"

"Been here a long time. The Book of Lavitticus—hit's in chapter nineteen or twenty—tells how the Lord commanded the Isrellites not to let their cattle breed with a differnt kind. But he must not of meant that be the case with their asses—donkeys—and their horses, 'cause they shore breeded them togather and made mules. Scriptures tell about David ridin' a mule, his boy Abslum ridin' a mule, and in the books of Sammel and Kings Solomon hisself ridin' a mule. There's lot of times mules was give to kings, and prophets ridin' a mule, or tellin' somebody to go and ride a mule."

"Never heerd tell none of that."

"Yep, Hershell. Hit's all right there in the Bible."

Looked to me like he could of saw I wasn't particular keen on listening at him, but he still wasn't ready to shut up.

"But I ain't never understood with mules bein' so handy to mankind why the Lord never made mules so they could have younguns theyselves. Ain't no such thing as a mule havin' a mule daddy and a mule mama. Reckon why that is?"

I started to ask him did the Good Book say anything about a prophet or king getting hisself kicked by one them Leviticus mules, but that might have kept him going even more.

I knowed then that man didn't stand no more

chance of making a crop by hisself than he would of flying some airplane.

They's something you can pretty well almost always count on seeing on a man what's, you know, kind of funny. Well, you take a look, remember what I'm saying: their hat don't never set right on their heads. From that morning on I never seen Uncle Mayfield with a hat on what wasn't golly-whumped on his head.

I asked him, "Uncle Mayfield, what you do for a living?"

"I retail jars of salves and bottles of liniments for ruematiss, croup, biles, medicinal purposes, Hershell, what I order through the mail." He reached up and scratched his head. "And I transport scrap iron to the ice plant on my Model T runabout, get ten cent a hunerd fer hit. Folks glad to get junk iron hauled off." I wondered why he didn't haul any of that junk he had on his own place.

Hit wasn't just farming. More'n that. Hit become plainer ever day I was there that manual labor wasn't Uncle Mayfield's cup of tea.

Not bragging, but Paw knowed what he was doing when they sent me. My paw larned me to do hard manual labor from the time I was one day old. And farming's second nature to a Mooneyham, which you sure better know before you take on them Flatwoods. And, praise be, Josie made up for Uncle Mayfield.

Like all Mooneyhams, she knowed hard work. Lean

as a razor, she was. She'd wrap a bandanna tight around her head, put on brogans, trousers, just like a man. And do more work than most any man.

We, that's mostly me and Josie altogether, went to work. We was up and out every day before the sun got up, and didn't go in until hit was red and halfway out of sight going down. Walking from the barn to the house our shadows'd be stretched out fifteen foot or more. That late in the day.

First off, with Jellie and Bean we busted up the cleared land and planted corn on hit. In planting corn you need to do hit when the moon's right (that's a Mooneyham family secret, ain't never been wrote down).

Then we taken on the uncleared land. With the shovels, crosscut saw, and axes we set to cutting blackgum and sweetgum saplings, digging up stumps, cutting and whacking down brush and vines, and then piling hit all up for burning. In five minutes sweat'd be sloshing out the top of my brogans.

One of them days, not long after I done moved in, we'd just stopped a minute to rest. I'd been swinging the kizer blade and Josie'd been piling brush and vines.

"Uncle May mighty keen on Bible readin', ain't he?" (I'd done quit calling him "Uncle Mayfield.")

"Lordy, yes."

"Course ain't nothin' wrong about that. All of us orter read it more. Most of us don't, though."

"Not him, Hershell. Mayfield not only kin tell you how many books in the Bible and name 'em all, he kin tell you how many chapters is in each book, and how many in the whole Bible. I declare, I believe he even knows how many verses in most of them chapters."

"I ain't ever heerd nobody, even no preachers, what knowed the Bible like that."

"They ain't none, Hershell."

"Like I say, ain't nothin' wrong with hit. But that shore seems to be all that's on his mind. Hard work ain't." Then I wished I hadn't said that last part.

But Josie just laughed. "The Bible's to him's like some big puzzle, seems like, that he just wants to study on all time." Then the Mooneyham come out in her, too. "Hit's also his way of showin' off. That ain't gone win him no poplairty contest."

Well, I thought I'd put a test to that. The next morning he had just dumped Jellie his eight corn ears in the stall trough, and I popped him: "Uncle May, how many books in the Old Testiment?"

"Thirty-nine."

"How about the New?"

"Twenty-six."

"You wouldn't happen to know how many chapters is in the Old Testiment?"

"Nine hunerd and thirty. Why you ast?"

THREE

Praise be, in them days we also happened on some help from a colored man—Sam Cook and his boy—when we was able to scratch up a little money.

Hit was early March that first year.

Me and Josie was hacking away with our kizers, I'd say not over seventy-five or a hundred foot off the public road. All around, everwheres, nothing but acres and acres covered in one big thicket. Tree saplings and sprouts, cockleburs, begger lice, vines and briars up to our ears, us not seeming to get nowheres, and me thinking of Pontotoc ridge where you hitch a pair of mules onto a plow, say, "Giddap!" and a middle buster just digs down and slices through the dirt, cutting the ground smooth, nice and easy. And you ain't got nothing to worry about except keeping a strong grip on the plow and making a straight row. Was we ever gonna see that day on this place?

Just then a sapling sprung back from Josie and a switch of stinging needle briars slapped me upside the face.

"Watch hit, Josie!"

I wiped my hand up across my face and seen blood on hit. I said some words what wasn't complimentry to them Flatwoods, but I ain't gonna write them down. Wondered how come I had to be the one Paw sent.

Then we seen this colored man and a strapping fourteen- or fifteen-year-old boy cross over the ditch to where we was at.

He tipped his hat (have you ever saw a colored man what went around bareheaded?): "Excuse me, Miss. But hit 'pears to me that you and the young gentleman might need some good hands."

"And what's your name?"

"Sam. Sam Cook, ma'am. This here is my boy Sillvestar." I larned later everbody called that boy "Snow." You can guess why.

"Where you all live, Sam?"

"About two mile from here over on Handle Mill Road. Everbody knows me, Miss."

"Sam, this here's hard, slow work. Ain't for no sissies."

"I knows that, Miss. That's all me and my boy here know. He's good a hand's me. Ain't no lazy bone in his body."

"When could you start?"

"Right now!"

"Naw. Tell you what, Sam. You and Sillvestar come back in the mornin', and we'll give hit a try. Be here by sunup."

"Yessum." And they left.

"Josie, you see them feet on Sillvestar?"

"He was barfooted."

"Yeah. Ain't them the widest feet you ever seen? And you see them long toes of his'n? Splayed out like fingers. That boy could roost in a tree."

Both was right there next morning, Johnny-on-the-spot with their water jugs. Josie give Sam an axe and Snow a kizer blade. We didn't have to tell them no more.

Josie broke off late that morning, and told us to be at the house at dinnertime. She taken hoecakes and made sandwiches out of hard fried eggs and streaks of lean. Two apiece for me, Sam, and Snow, and a baked sweet tater. And hot coffee.

Sam did some tall bragging on Josie's cooking, allowing how he never had et no better sandwiches.

About sundown we broke off for the day, and Josie give Sam a dollar. "I'm willin' to give you and Sillvestar half dollar a day apiece when we need you."

"Thank you, Miss Josie. Reckon you might be needin' us tomorrer?"

"Yes, Sam, we can use you for the next couple days."

When they left Josie was shore hating that we didn't have but a little over three dollars in the house. But, as luck would have it, that very week Josie opened a letter from Mama and in hit was a twenty-dollar bill. Ain't no telling how long Mama'd been saving up to get it.

Late Friday Josie told Sam, "Sam, I'm fixin' to put a lot of trust in you. We want you and Sillvestar to come back next week, and I'm fixin' to pay you in advance five dollars."

"Lord bless you, Miss Josie! You kindest person I ever knowed!"

"Well, now, that ain't exactly all they is to hit, Sam. I want a promise out of you."

"Anything you say, Miss Josie!"

"I want you to take Sillvestar over to the county seat tomorrer and git him a pair of shoes."

"Oh, praise be, Miss Josie! I cain't think of nothin' I'd druther do. No, ma'am. Nothin'."

When they come back Monday morning, Snow was all grins. His britches was rolled halfway to his knees. He had on a pair of shiny high-top brown brogans what laced part the way up, the last three hooks. His was hooked all the way to the top.

"Them's 'Peters' shoes, Miss Josie. Come from Hill's Department Store! Sho' did. Mr. Roy D. Hill's a mighty fine gentleman! When he seen Sillvestar he come up from the back office and told them ladies he'd wait on Sillvestar. Mr. Roy had to do some huntin', but finally found a pair what fit Sillvestar. Just right. And he thowed in two pair of sox, all for $3.75."

Snow standing there, just grinning. Then Sam got to laughing: "Taken him all day yesteday to larn how to tie 'em. You know, Miss Josie and Mr. Hershell, I was skeered that boy might buck hisself to death when we put them shoes on him!"

"Oh, Sam!"

"Yes, ma'am, Miss Josie! Sho' did!" Sam spun around, bent over double, stomped his foot, slapped his hands on his legs, then straightened up and busted out laughing: "That ain't all. He backed off in the creek lookin' at his tracks."

Ain't no telling how long them shoes lasted. But to this good day I don't know if old Sam was joshing Josie and me or not.

When Sam and Snow was working in tandem, like aholt of a crosscut saw, or the two of them hacking away with their axes digging up a oak stump, most always you'd hear 'em singing and a-humming, "Come—on—, little Mo-ses, come—on! Ummm-mm-m-uh! Come—on—, little Mo-ses, come—on! Ummm-mmm-m-uh!" Or some such. And that saw or them axes would go along in time. Me and Josie got to where we'd join in, and sometimes we'd even do one of their spirituals when hit was just me and her working. "Oh-h-h Lord Jee-sus, do have mer-cy on me!" Sam and Snow could make you almost forget that what you was doing was mighty slow, and mighty hard labor.

FOUR

Summers was hot. You may think you know what hit's like being hot, but wait till you try farming Flatwoods land in July and August. And winters just as cold as summers hot.

Anyways, after fighting 'skeeters and coming down with malarial fever ever summer and hacking croup and flu ever winter, in four year we'd done cleared and fenced a little over sixty-five acres. I even picked out a spot of ground with a low trough, borrowed a slip, and me and Jelly and Bean with Sam's and Snow's help made a levee bank holding a little more than a one-and-a-half-acre pond in our twenty-two acre pasture. Hit ain't never went dry, neither. (Almost did one or two year, like in 19 and 30, but never quite.) We had crab-grass, dallis grass, some Bermuda and johnson grass, lespedeza, all pretty well crowding out the bitterweeds, and good grazing and hay for the mules, milk cow, and steers—any livestock we was raising.

And we added on two and a half rooms to their house, new galvanized tin roof, and dog trot hall. We got well water at twenty-seven feet, and had soft rain-water from a two-hundred-fifty-gallon cistern. That was another thing Sam and Snow was handy at. They'd dig and clean out wells. Ain't many men anxious to get down in one them wells.

Hit wasn't long after I got there I could of told my folks there was something else what liked that old wet land with all them vines, stumps, and saplings: snakes and rabbits.

Chicken snakes, blue racers, king snakes, spreading adders, wasn't nothing to see one them ever day a-scurrying away. Copperheads and water moccasins, too, ever week or so. Rattlers wasn't no stranger to them Flatwoods. Wasn't nothing to have to kill one or two of 'em ever year. One year I kilt had seven rattles. Them snakes was another reason (if'n he'd of needed one) Uncle May was scarce outside the house.

I larned that about him the first summer. Another bothersome thing to farmers is field rats getting in their corncribs. Ain't no way to build a crib what'll keep 'em out. Many's the time I've had to stomp a rat soon's I stepped in the crib. Some of 'em ain't all that scared of you, neither, you done got him cornered—I've heard of folks getting bit by a rat.

Cats in the barn can help some, but you get a couple of sowcats, soon you'll hear 'em frolicking up in the loft with some tomcat and first thing you know rats might be scarcer, ain't that many rats, but you got a lot more cats. And I never was one to put a litter of kittens in a croker sack and go drown 'em.

Paw always seen that he had a chicken snake in the crib. Hit'll lay there on the corn or wrapped around a joist, and late summer hit'll burrow under the shucks and stay in the crib on into the fall. Then, most times, come back in early spring. A chicken snake'll keep rats out of a corncrib better'n anything I know. The bigger that snake's the better.

Hit's one more sight to see one of 'em swaller'n a rat whole. He done got that rat with one big snap of them jaws, and in the rat starts, hits head going in first. When he gets past them jaws that snake'll go to swelling out twict, three, maybe four times hits natural size—that rat still a-kicking. You gonna think that sucker's gonna choke shore'n hell. Set there and watch, though, and by and by you'll finally see the tail of that rat go plumb out of sight. Chicken snake ain't one bit of bother, neither.

So naturally, when I seen a big old chicken snake aside the path one morning in late spring, I didn't kill hit but taken him to the barn, laid him in the crib, and went on back to the field. Didn't say nothing to nobody 'cause didn't think nothing about hit.

Late in the evening, wasn't over two, three days

later when I come in from the field, Josie, she run out the house and met me going in the barn lot.

"Hershell, you put that snake in the barn?"

"Yeah."

"I thought so. You got to get shed of hit!"

"Why?"

"Jest a while ago I told Mayfield to go out and shuck some corn ears and put them in the stalls for the mules, and he seen that snake kiled up in the crib."

"Whyn't he jest shoo him away?"

"Shoo hit away? *Him* shoo a snake away? Hershell, a dead snake'll break Mayfield out in a rash."

"I never thought about him bein' afeared of a damn chicken snake."

I seen her laughing. "Hershell, you know what he done when he seen that snake?" She turned her head away, and then turned back to me, this time serious. "Naw, hit's too embarrsin'."

And, talking about them rabbits, Sam and Snow larned me something. What they done, they taken a solid stick—oak or hickory—about two foot long, and stuck a big iron nut they'd picked up from the machinery shop over at the county seat on hits end. That's what they chunked at rabbits. One or two fellers'd stand on one side of a brush pile and another'd shake a bush or kick brush on t'other side. Any rabbit in there shore gonna run out. Wasn't long after I tried my hand at hit I got to where I never needed to waste no shotgun shells.

Like most folks what hunt together, we become buddies. Sam always let me throw first. "Mr. Hershell," Sam'd say, "ain't a nigger in the county can beat you killin' rabbits with that stick." And I ain't bragging, but if that rabbit come splitting out on my side, no matter how fast, no matter the crooks and turns he made, hits chances was slim to nothing whenever I throwed my stick. Ker-thump! and for that rabbit twenty-three skidoo. I even knowed when he was about to change direction.

My knife stays sharp enough to shave 'cause I always carry a whetrock. Don't take me no time to clean a rabbit. Just slice through the fur and skin to hits flesh on hits back. Then, with one hand on one side of the gash and another hand on t'other, strip hits hide all off head to tail. Then you slice under hits belly, and yank hits guts out. I can skin, gut, and cut up a rabbit into two hind and two front legs and back, and have hit ready for a skillet or pot in less the time than hit's taken me to tell this.

We had fried rabbits, rabbit stews, parboiled rabbits, and rabbit dumplings. Any ways there is to cook a rabbit Josie knowed hit. Only one thing you got to remember about rabbits, don't eat one in warm weather. They wormy then. Wait till after the first frost.

And I tell you, coming in about dark on a freezing

day, all shaking, and then frying up a couple of fresh-kilt rabbits with thick brown gravy, biscuits big as hoe-cakes covered in melted butter, and hot coffee black as an African, that ain't bad. They's a lot worser eating than that.

FIVE

By the by, they's something else I taken with me to Uncle May's and Aunt Josie's. Ain't proud of hit; ain't all that ashamed, neither. Anyways, I filled a Mason jar of Paw's likker out his jug. Being a Mooncyham, Paw believed in keeping a dram handy. That was a subject he never seen fit to talk to Mama about, 'cause Mama, like ever decent woman I ever knowed, she was dead set against likker. In church young gals are all time standing up and proclaiming: "The lips that tetch likker will *never* tetch mine!" So Paw never taken no likker in the house, but did keep his jug, stoppered good with a corncob, covered over in the back corner of the crib. On cold days he might take a snort, and around Christmas he was shore gonna make hisself a few eggnogs.

Paw told me: "I ain't tellin' you to drink likker, son,

and ain't tellin' you not to. That'll be your business. Ef'n you do, though, they's some things I am tellin' you. Remember, first off, likker ain't nothin' to play 'round with, get you in trouble faster'n anything I know of. They's times you might be offered a drink by somebody tryin' to be polite or friendly, and he could figger you high-hattin' him or consider'n yourself better'n him ef'n you turn him down. But don't never take more'n that one drink with air man you don't know or don't trust. Likker and bad company are dynamite. Pintentry's full of men who never would of been there—and graveyards, too, as soon as they was—without likker and bad company. And don't never take no drink when you're mad or upset, or when you air worried about somethin'. Likker don't add the first brain in your head, and'll make whatever made you mad or's troubling you a heap sight worser.

"Everthing else you'll need to know about likker," Paw said, "you'll larn soon enough on your own."

Paw never told me, but I knowed hit was against the law to sell likker, or even to keep a dram for yourself. When I got a little older that put me to studying: why was hit against the law?

Mr. Charley Lomax, the barber what cut my hair, and me talked about hit. Course that wasn't all we talked about. You never knowed when you went in Mr. Charley's shop what the subject might be, except you knowed he wasn't short on information on anything. And wasn't no need to try and change a subject until he got through telling you everthing he done decided you oughta know on hit.

I went to Mr. Charley's barbershop mainly on account of his tub. Onct a month (if I had the money) I taken a bath there. His tub was longer'n the other two shops', and you always knowed Shine (Shine Tittle shined shoes for them what had the dime to spare—that's why they called him "Shine") kept the tub clean—never seen no rings in that tub—and their hot water heater stoked and you was gonna have plenty of hot *running* water, a big bar store-bought Ivory soap what floated on top the water where's you could always see it, and two clean towels. A bathtub shore beats a washtub. No kettle or pans to heat on the kitchen range, or when you through having to tote the tub out the back door to empty hit. Mr. Charley charged two bits for the bath, two bits for a shave, and another two bits for the haircut, six bits all told. All together that's a pretty good piece of change. I went weekdays mostly 'cause then most of the time wouldn't be nobody in there but Mr. Charley and Shine. Excepting when a customer'd wandered in.

Mr. Charley's shop had two chairs, but the other one was used only on Saturday, the busy day, when Amos Lancaster helped out.

Mr. Amos was a big cutup.

"Mornin', Marshal!" Mr. Charley folded his newspaper and got up out of his barber's chair when Sam Davis, the town marshal, walked in just ahead of me.

The marshal taken a seat. Mr. Charley put a face towel around his neck, and pinned the apron on him. "Put hit tight, Charley, don't want no hair gettin' down my neck."

Mr. Charley grunted.

"And watch that mole back of my neck. Try not to cut hit off this time."

Mr. Charley didn't laugh.

Shine brung his stool over to the barber chair, taken a rag out and begun cleaning the marshal's shoes. Mr. Charley taken his clippers off the shelf behind him and started on the marshal's hair.

"Where's Amos?"

"He don't come in excep' Satdays, Marshal."

Marshal told him that's right, he knowed that.

"Don't believe I could handle Amos ever day."

"Stirs you up, huh?"

"Hell, yeah. He don't figger he's livin' unlessen he's pullin' some prank or kiddin' somebody. Don't make one damn who 'tis, neither!"

"Don't have to tell me about Amos."

"Sometimes I think me'n him gotta part compny, but I happen to need Amos more'n he needs me. Charley Lomax ain't the man to cut off his nose to spite his face. He's best barber in the county, bar none, and Amos can cut a head of hair in less'n five minutes. On Satdays that comes in handy. But damned if he can't make me mad.

"Old man Sprayberry come in Satday about four

weeks ago. Mr. *Fetherstone Walthall* Sprayberry. You know Mr. Feb's ever bit of seventy. He been postmaster for at least thirty of 'em, and me nor you, neither, never seen him outside that post office without his hat on, or when he wadn't wearin' a suit and tie. And you know how nice and polite he always is. A one hunerd percent gentleman, through and through."

"What'd Amos do?"

"Mr. Sprayberry come in, taken off his hat, hung hit over there on the rack. 'Good morning, Mr. Lomax, Mr. Lancaster.' Then he turned to the customers and said, 'How you gentlemen?'

"There was nods and 'Hello, Mr. Feb.'

"'Nice day, ain't it?'" He taken his seat there on the bench.

"Nods from them on the bench again, and he set there waiting his turn. When Amos hollered out 'Next!' and the old man's turn come he got up to git in Amos's chair. "And how's Mrs. Lancaster these days, Amos?" he ast. Amos told him fine.

"Well, sir, just when Mr. Fetherstone Walthall Sprayberry—the first elder in our First Prespeterun Church—set hisself down in Amos's chair, out of the blue come the damndest fart. You coulda heerd it out in the street. Skeered the living shit out of me when I seen I'd damn near cut a customer I was shavin'."

"That musta broke up the crowd."

"Naw, now. Not right off it didn't. Mr. Feb he turned red. Pertendin' nothin' happened but could tell he was embarrassed. Shop full of customers, and hit shore was hard to do, but out of respect for him everbody stayed quiet. Then Mr. Feb, he shifted around in the chair and out come another fart! A squealing one! Seein' who hit was what had just let them farts, they just couldn't hold it no longer. Everbody busted out laughin'."

Marshal grinned. "Reckon what Feb had ate?"

"Naw, Marshal, what hit was, that damned Amos had done slipped one them fartin' pillers in the seat just before Mr. Sprayberry set his ass on it."

"What'd Sprayberry say?"

"He taken it well. Even old man Feb, when he seen what hit was, got tickled."

"You could have had yourself a problem, Charley. Sprayberry ain't like most folks. You know he's a Republican. Votes that way in ever presdental race."

"Marshal, you orter know why. Voting Republican's how he got his job. In my lifetime ain't been no Demcrat presdent other'n Woodrow Wilson until last year when Franklin D. won. I 'spect you'd vote Republican, too, to git yourself a job like his. Teddy Roosevelt give him his."

"Hell, naw, I wouldn't. Ain't nothin'd make me vote for no damn Republican. Nothin'."

Mr. Charley laughed. "I ain't about to dispute the town marshal. At least they don't have no trouble countin' the Republican votes. Anybody besides Mr. Feb and his old lady what votes Republican does hit by mistake."

Mr. Charley put his scissors back on the shelf. "See some of Mister Dan Druff's boys been visiting, Marshal. You want the Fitch's or Lucky Tiger?"

"Let's try the Tiger, Charley."

"That orter do the trick. Lucky Tiger's got witch hazel in hit. Got a growl—hah-hah!"

Mr. Charley dashed on the tonic and went to rubbing away on the marshal's head. "Anyways, I told him later, 'Amos, I swear you goner run off ever *good* customer I got. Don't you know no better'n pullin' a stunt like that on a dignified old man like Mr. Feb?'"

"You ain't goner change Amos, Charley."

"No. I give up on him long ago. But now wait, he did git tit for tat last Satday. And from a kid, at that."

"Let's hear it."

"When Amos is cuttin' some kid's hair—more timid the kid is the better—along about the time when he's gettin' through and lettin' him out of the chair, he's just liable to ast the chap if he'd like to make a nickel. Course they ain't nairn who don't. Then Amos tells him he'll give him a nickel to show him his 'talleywhacker.' Genrally the kid turns red, don't know what to say—some look like they about to cry—and Amos has hisself a big laugh."

"Grown man shouldn't do no kid like that."

Mr. Charley was stropping his razor. "Naw. Course not. Kids that age mighty senstive about their ding-dongs. Worried if hit's big enough. Or shaped natral, or way hit's s'posed to look. Now when a man's along about thirty-five or forty, genrally—I say *genrally*—anyways them what's got any sense—hit begins sinkin' in his head what the most overrated thing in the world is, and that's screwin', and the most underrated thing in the world is a good crap. Then he's worryin' about his bowel movements instead that particler part of his anatmy. But not kids. And kids mighty private, too, don't want nobody else lookin' at hit.

"Course, Amos, he knowed all that.

"But his ass had a comeuppance last Satday. I know you know 'Watermelon' Buchanan's boys?" (They called him 'Watermelon' 'cause he growed watermelons and peddled them ever summer on the court square.)

"Oh, yeah. Fister and Bays."

"Well, this was Fister. That kid cain't be no more'n ten or twelve, is he? And Amos had been cuttin' Fister's hair, was lettin' him out of the chair and just about to call out 'Next!' when he taken that damn notion. So he said, real nice: 'Son, would you like to make a nickel?'

"Shop packed full. Ears perked up, 'specially them that knowed what was comin'.

"'Oh, yessir!'

"'Well,' he told him, 'tell you what. I'll give you a nickel,' and acting like he was whisperin' but loud a plenty so everbody heerd it, 'to let me see your talleywhacker.'

"Fister stepped on down out of the chair, turned

around. Then he stopped, and stood there. You coulda heerd a pin drop.

"'All right. I'm fixin' to show hit to you. And you're a *lie-ing son of a bitch* ef you don't gimme that nickel.'

"Everbody in the shop howled. One customer fell off the bench. After that, whenever one would leave, he'd say, 'So long, Mr. Charley,' and then real solemn, 'and so long to you, too, MR. TALLERWHACKER!' Old Amos shet his ass up for the rest of the day."

But getting back to the point. I been meaning to tell you about our talk on the likker law.

When the marshal left, me'n Mr. Charley got off on hit.

"Looks to me like they'd repeal the likker law, Mr. Charley."

"Ain't goner happen, Hershell."

"Why? Lawmen don't never try to enforce hit except agin' niggers and pore white trash."

"Preachers and bootleggers. Bootleggers don't want to repeal it 'cause they'd be out of business, and preachers, they listening to the women and bluenoses."

"Bluenoses?"

"Yep. You *know* bluenoses. Them's folks what think they religious when they ain't nothin' but bilius. Now I don't believe in talkin' about folks, but take old Kelsie Dinsmore. Settin' there cashier of First State Bank, he'd see you starve and never blink a eye. Cold-blooded as a lamper eel. On Sundays he'll be in church on that second row all shaved and starched, frownin' and solemn as Solomon. Thinks the only way to be religious is to be uncomforble. He ain't never taken a drink and don't never intend to, and thinks you orter die and go to Hell ef *you* do. Fact is, his kind thinks 99 percent of the human race is going to a burnin' Hell, anyways, and don't bother them one bit they air—hit's jest what they deserve. I tell you, Hershell, Kelsie Dinsmore's a man I wouldn't take no drink with even ef that sonabitch drank."

"But what about them that do like a little snort? They's plenty of them."

"Oh, hell, yes. Don't mean to talk about nobody—ain't none my business—but take Mr. Jessie Armstead gits his out of Memphis. No wildcat for him. Bottled in bond. Green label. 'Ole Taylor' or 'Ole Grandad,' one hunderd proof. They mighty quiet about hit, but him and his wife both likes their nip."

He looked to see for sure Shine wasn't nowheres around: "They maid tells Shine all about 'em. But, like you say, the likker law don't cause them no problem. Law ain't about to bother the man what owns the Farmers and Merchants Bank, 'specially for no more than having his own private bottle. And Mr. Jessie and Miss Rose just don't see no pint in contrarying they preacher about no likker law."

"Ain't that being kind of hippie-crittle?"

"Why, shore, Hershell. How many folks you think'd

be in churches on Sundays ef the hippie-crits stayed home?"

"I know Senator Titcomb ever election year tells everbody he believes in having a strong likker law, and how his arm'd wither off like Jeroboam's afore he holds hit up to repeal hit."

"That pussy-footin' Lamar Titcomb! He knows that's goner suit the women, preachers, and bluenoses, and the law don't never bother them that takes a drink on the sly, includin' him, none."

"You mean to say with all that talk Senator Titcomb drinks hisself?"

"My lordamighty, Hershell! He'd git the blue ribbon for bein' the biggest hippie-crit of 'em all! You never taken a good look at him? Skippin' around at them grand round speakin's, runnin' for the state senate, and yellin', 'Pro-high-bishun, PRO-HIGH-BISHUN, PRO-HIGH-BISHUN!' Ever take a look at them eyeballs of his'n? They red as a fox's ass in pokeberry season."

"Mr. Charley, shorely the preachers ain't hippie-crits theyselves, air they?"

"Naw, Hershell, the preachers is one set of folks, at least, what ain't hippie-crits. They ain't got no doubts atall about the likker law. Leastwise most of 'em ain't. They truly believe they doing the good Lord's work. You right about that."

I was about to say something, but he wasn't through.

"But that's worser, 'cause they ain't no arguin' with air man what's got hit in his head deep down he's doin' what the Lord tells him."

"Ain't sure I'm following you, Mr. Charley—"

"Hershell, some the damndest fool things ever been did was by folks with good intentions. And, 'specially, 'specially them's what ain't got no doubts hit's the Lord telling them what to do. Likker law's just one sample."

"They that bad, huh?"

"Give me a damn rascal any day to one of them."

When he said that, hit brung to mind something hid way back of my head I tried to keep hid.

My mama brung me up, and ever preacher I heard talk preached that everthing wrote in the Bible happened just the way hit was wrote down, i for i, tittle for tittle, jot for jot, and the worsest sin a pore soul could commit was to doubt anything wrote in the Holy Writ.

Hit shaken me all inside what I couldn't no more help than breathe.

I respected Mr. Charley so much, right next to my paw, and I wanted help from him now more'n anybody I knowed. But I wisht I never asked him that one thing.

"Mr. Charley, you ain't—you ain't got air doubt but what everthing wrote in the Holy Bible is exactly so, have you?"

"Hell, yes, I got doubts, plenty of 'em."

"My lordamighty. Good lordamighty, that makes you one them infidels, don't it?"

"Don't know what a infidel is, Hershell, don't give a whittler's damn, neither. Hershell, like your paw, Mr. Tolbert, I been around, have saw folks all my life."

He had plenty more to say.

"Hershell, far's I'm concerned a man can believe air thing he wants to, that there's his business, none a mine. I shore ain't goner argue with him. Hit's when he comes in my shop telling me what I got to believe. That's when he done crossed the line."

He'd done stopped cutting my hair.

"Hershell, ever man got to find his own way to them pearly gates. Since I only got halfway through the fifth grade I ain't all that much on readin'. But I do read in the Bible time to time, shore do, probly not as much as I should, but I do read the Bible, and I know men or women wiser'n I'll ever be wrote. And, yes, I believe God Almighty must have had a hand in what's wrote."

He come in front of the chair, scissors in one hand, comb in t'other.

"But Hershell, I don't have to open that sacret Bible layin' all day in my house to see the hand of Jesus Christ at work.

"Least three or four times a year I see it right here in my shop.

"I've saw men the meanest sonsofbitches in the county. Whup they wives, beat they kids, stay half drunk, wife and kids beggars out on the streets. Yank out they pocketknife at some 'tonk, open hit up, and cut the guts out some feller what hadn't done nothin' to them. Dread to see one of 'em come in the shop. You scared of that sneaky bastard.

"Then one day, Hershell, he comes in the shop, and he ain't here more'n a few minutes you see you're lookin' at a entirely different man.

"You larn later him and some preacher—may have big time one, but maybe a preacher nobody knows much about, but a preacher—them two meet up somehow. You may hear about hit from someone else. Or, *he* could be the one to tell—not braggin' or boastin'—just straight out tellin' you matter-of-fact like.

"Anyways, him and that preacher, the two of them talk. Set there and talk. Maybe pray. Hit may be you cain't tell what that man's thinkin', him just settin' there straight-faced, but him and that preacher holdin' hands like two childern . . .

"And sometimes that sorry bastard what hadn't shed a tear in thirty year starts into crying. Tears comes out like Niegrer Falls and he lays there, his head on the shoulders of that preacher, shakin' and sobbin', wailin'.

"Later, he don't try to make no show of hit. Don't have to. He never takes a swaller of whiskey rest of his life. Never lays a hand in anger on his wife or kids. Him, his wife, and they childern settin' in church ever Sunday mornin'. Case of fire or sickness at some neighbor's, he's first one there tryin' to help out. Widder women, orphans.

"What changed that man, Hershell? Only a damn fool'd try to explain hit.

"But gettin' back to whether I believe everthing what's wrote in the Bible happened just the way hit's wrote down, naw, I don't.

"Ain't got no hang-up about preachers, give 'em credit for wanting to make the world better.

"But bein' a preacher ain't no garntee from bein' a damn fool, also. I've saw some preachers' eyes so close togather if he happened to fall on a nail hit'd put both his eyes out.

"Now take them mirkles you supposed to believe, no doubt, that is ef you want to git to Heaven . . . Some would have been okay, I guess, like Jesus feeding over five thousand folks with a handful of fish. Nice, but I don't see where you believe that did or did not happen makes air difference with Jesus.

"Then they's two more, one I believe Jesus'd be disapinted to think you figgered was so, and another I can tell you straight out never happened.

"Take His first mirkle, Jesus changing water to wine. Some our Baptists claim hit was grape juice, but the Bible said hit was wine, not no ordnary wine neither, but good kind, the kind served when compny first arrived. Not what you serve when they done drank enough not to know no differnce."

"What's wrong with that, Mr. Charley?"

"My God, Hershell, don't hit seem strange to you that Jesus Christ would use some awesome power no human's got jest so some folks at a party could stay half geed up a while longer?

"Now, les take another mirkle I can tell you right now never happened. You remember Lazrus and his two sisters, Martha and Mary?"

"Shore."

"Well, you know Jesus went to they house after Lazrus was dead. Three, four days, warn't hit? His body'd began to stink.

"Well, here come Martha and Mary, runnin' out sobbin' to Jesus their brother was dead and beggin' him to bring Lazrus back to this life. And, *accordin' to scriptures,* Jesus brung him back. Lazrus got up out that coffin.

"Now, Hershell, I ain't doubtin' one minute but they ast Jesus this. But, ef they done that, do you know what Jesus would have said?"

"Nawsir, I shore don't, Mr. Charley."

"He would of said, 'Air you two women nuts? Bring Lazrus from where he is right now to this here earth—here of all places—just because his two sisters are boohooing and miss him? He'd want to wring both your necks. You crazy girls.'

"Accordin' to scriptures Jesus come to this earth to save the lost human race. Almost two thousand year done gone. Jesus is shore takin' His time ef that's what the Holy Writ meant for us to unnerstand.

"More mixed-up folks tellin' us what we got to believe to git through them pearly gates. Baptists and

Camelites—call theyselves Church of Christ now—say you got to be dunked plumb out of sight in some creek or pond. Methdists and Presbyteruns say a half cup of water poured on your head'll do the trick. Primtive Baptists wash one another's feet. Church of Christ folks say you cain't have no pianner or organ playin in church when they sing praises to the Lord, sinnin' I guess ef'n you do. Get in squabble, all of 'em. Arguin' over things seem to me don't make a tinker's damn.

"Hershell, bein' a Christian don't mean you got to chunk all the sense you got out the winder. Why did the Good Lord give us a brain ef'n he never meant for us to use it?"

He stopped, I thought, finally, but he studied a bit. "Hershell, you know Mr. Patrick Hennessey, that fine man what sells life insurance?"

"Yes, sir."

"Well, about twenty-five or thirty year ago him and his fine little famly moved here into our county. Some our Freemason brethern and high-class Baptist deacons larned somethin' awful about him. Hit was whispered he was one them *Cathlics*. So they had theyselves a settee onct they knowed that was so, and formed a delegation to call on Mr. Hennessey and politely suggest to him might be better ef him and his famly moved elsewhere.

"Somehow one man, one man heerd about hit—Mr. Joe Lowry—and he had the guts to go tell them they had done lost ever brain in their heads. Mr. Joe told 'em,

'Leave Mr. Hennessey alone, you goddamnned idiots.' And that ended that."

Like I said, Mr. Charley never stopped until he'd covered the whole bolt of cloth on ever subject he'd begun to talk on.

I got out of his chair, give him three quarters what he rung up in his little cash register.

"I ain't one to gossip." He leant over next to my ear. "But that ain't all their maid tells Shine. Mr. Jessie whups up on Miss Rose some them Satday nights. Some so bad's why she ain't in church the next day."

Then he taken a seat back in his chair what I'd just got out of.

SIX

Getting back to Uncle May. Like I said, he was a one-man longitude on religious stuff. Somehow or 'nother he'd scratched together enough money to buy hisself a radio. Hit was run by a battery; we didn't have no electricity. Uncle May knowed ever preacher that could be heard on hit. Listened at them ever day. Might be that radio station down at Kosciusko, or plumb out to them stations far away as Del Rio, Texas, and El Dorado, Arkansas. Never figured why the Kosciusko station no more'n ninety mile away always made such a staticky racket. Lots of times I couldn't hardly stand to be around when hit was on, and them other stations what was so far away most of the time was as plain as somebody talking in the next room. Del Rio had a guitar player—they called him "Pass the Biskits, Pappy"—who them folks in Texas finally made governor. Also had a medical doctor what sewed goat glands in old men that made them young and frisky again (so he claimed). Didn't never tell what hit did to that goat.

At noon we'd come in out the field, sun blazing hot like a skillet, sweat stinging your eyes. After we'd done et, I always taken my shoes off and laid out on the porch. I'd still be tired and aching, trying to rest a bit, scratching my feet on the posts and dreading going back to them clods.

But Uncle May? He wasn't sweating. No, sir. He'd be setting there in a straight chair, hat on and shirt collar buttoned, and with them dollar specs he'd got from Doc Parker, the spec peddler, that'd give you a splitting headache to look through two minutes, reading some religious tract or booklet. They come through the mail in droves. Stacks and stacks of papers lying around all over the house. In ever corner and out in the hall they'd be piled up.

Ever now and then he might say to hisself, "This here is right. Brother Loper knows what he's talkin' about." But times I'd hear his teeth grinding, look around and see his old rooster-comb hair get redder and him muttering something like, "Don't this Spivens preacher know he ain't scriptural? He don't know goat turds from butterbeans."

And woe be some passerby when we was in the field if he stopped and Uncle May got started on him about religion. He'd stand there and talk at the man till dark, his head bobbing and jerking, if the feller didn't have no more sense than to stand there and listen at him. Uncle May'd never have made a crop by hisself even if he knowed how.

Now, Mr. Oscar Ivey, our mail carrier, considered hisself a Bible scholar. So him and Uncle May, they'd have at hit time to time.

One morning them two was out at the mailbox. Aunt Josie hollered for me to get Uncle May on down to the field.

Mr. Oscar had just tapped and opened his can of Rooster snuff. Pinched hisself a dip, pulled his bottom lip out and dropped hit in. "Well, Mayfield, you got to say farming is the Lord's work. Hard as farming is, farmers bound to be His favorite people."

"I don't know about that, Oscar."

"They ain't? Why?"

"The Book of Gensis. Read your scriptures, Oscar. Cain was the first farmer, and the Lord didn't 'specially care for his offerin'. Remember that? That's what brought on the trouble between him and Abel."

"Well, now, come to think of it, that is right, Mayfield. You right there."

"Let me ast you something else, Oscar."

"Shoot."

"Now anybody can understand Cain gettin' mad and jallous of Abel when the Lord favored him. What ain't clear to me is why the Lord took a likin' for somethin' that was kilt over somethin' growed. Can you tell me that?"

"I better git along and git this mail out."

Uncle May, he liked that.

When we was growing up, Mama read from the Bible to us children just about ever night. But now I never did try and figure out this religious stuff, too deep for me. And I shore didn't care nothing about hearing all Uncle May wanted to talk about. But didn't want to contrary him, neither, and the way I done that was just leave him alone and not show any interest in his palaver. Which wasn't hard to do.

Except one time—one time (when I was sort of feeling my oats) I did try to stir him a bit. I knowed better.

We was out on the porch. Me and Josie'd hoed hard and steady on one them clammy hot days, keeping the grass from taking over our young corn. And did a good job. We'd just et supper.

They's a special warm kind of feeling comes over a man after a hard day's manual labor, and he's washed hisself up, et a good supper, topped off with a cup of hot coffee, and he sets down to sort things out in his head.

Shadows from the chinaberry tree across the road had reached the porch.

I set down, taken out my sack of Golden Grain and rolled myself a cigarette. Felt a little breeze. Struck a match, lit up, and taken a good deep draw. Then I seen a nail laying on the floor. I picked hit up, looked over at Uncle May.

"Seems to me you allus talkin' in riddles."

"Riddles?"

"Yep. Riddles."

He set there. "Well, everthing is riddles, Hershell. Didn't you know that?"

I didn't say nothing.

"We dont know the 'why' to anything. A human cain't answer 'WHY' to nothing. Look at that nail you just picked up, Hershell."

I taken a look. Wasn't nothing but a six-penny nail.

"Let me ast you: Why is hit you can drive a nail in a board?"

Now wasn't that was a fool queston? I didn't try to answer.

"Well?"

"'Cause a nail is harder'n wood, that's why."

"Well, why is a nail harder'n wood?"

"Because a nail is made outa steel. Anybody knows that."

"Why is steel harder'n wood?"

"Because steel is made outa iron, and that's metal, and that's harder'n wood. Hit's that simple. You orter understand that."

"Well, tell me why metal is harder'n wood then?"

"Because hit just is, dammit!" I slang that nail down. "A nail's harder'n wood, and that's that!"

He wasn't ruffled.

"You see, Hershell, you thought you knowed why but now you really dint. You and me tryin' to answer 'why' to anything is like goin' up to some door what has 'ANSWER' wrote on hit. And so you open that door, but—lo and behold—the room's empty. Then on t'other side of the room they's another door with 'ANSWER' wrote on hit, and you say, 'Well, the answer's gotta be there,' and so you go and open that door. But you just opened the door to another empty room. One empty room after the other. Hershell, hit's like playin' 'Pin the tail on the donkey'" (then he done a 'hee-haw') "exceptin' only when they take the blindfold off *they ain't even no donkey there*."

On he palavered.

"You see, Hershell, we are M-O-R-T-A-L-I-T-I-E-S." (He spelled hit for me like the library lady done—"herpatology.") "All mortalities can do is mortalize." (Spelled that, too.) "And when a mortality mortalizes there is a fog, a wall, you might say. He may not even know hit's there, but he cain't never git past hit. And what he thinks is answers is only mortalizations."

He taken off his specs. "They cain't help lookin', but the most important things they is to know, no mortal never will know. Leastwise, not on this airth."

I never heard such fool talk. I should have shut up.

"Tell me somethin'. You git whut you're tellin' me out the Bible? Where does hit say all that what you're sayin'?"

"The Book of Gensis, Hershell. Remember the Lord

tellin' Adam to stay away from the Tree of Knowledge? Jehovah said, 'They's things, Adam, you ain't meant to know.' Then there was that Tower of Babel humans tried to build where's they could know everthing. The Lord stopped that, tore that tower down. Even old Job, as good a man as ever lived, had to be told by the Lord, 'Job, they's things you ain't got no business even tryin' to unnerstand.' Just like you cain't never larn old Mabel, our Jersey cow, to add and subtrack, they's things humans'll never know neither. I ain't puttin' humans down, Hershell, not one little bit. We smarter'n all the animals. Some human figgered out that radio we listen at somebody talkin' five hunderd mile away. Some human figgered out how just one gallen of gas kin move a car twenty mile. But what I am sayin' is out there is a great mystery ain't no human ever goner learn, and we ain't never goner learn why, leastwise not on this airth. That's what the Lord told Adam, and He ain't never changed His mind."

And finally, "But whatever answers *they is that's meant for us to know* is in this Book. Somers. Leastwise I don't know no better place to look."

He was setting there staring at me. Damn! Give him a ear and he'd talk you to death! Like I said, I ain't one to talk about religion. Mama read from hit to us children most ever night, but the Bible shore ain't my cup of tea. I was already uncomfortable. But here we was, neck deep.

I guess I just got mad and didn't have no more

sense than to give him another whack: "You've did a lot of talkin' about riddles. The Bible what my mama read to us childern made everthing plain. Hit warn't no mystery. Why cain't hit be that ways with you? You allus coming up with a riddle like what I heerd you tell Mr. Oscar. Ain't never heerd you give no answer."

"You want one with a answer?"

"I shore do."

Off he set. "Hershell, I 'spect Miss Gertrude read to you childern about Abraham, Isaac, Jacob? Jacob and Esau was Isaac's and Rebekah's twin childern. You remember them?"

I nodded.

"Jacob had been livin' and workin' for years for his daddy-in-law, Laban. Laban was Rebekah's brother. Jacob wanted to go home. So, here he was headed back to Hebron with his two wives, Leah and Rachel, and their childern. Now that Jacob was one more trickster, and he had did old Laban dirty. He had slipped off with sheep and goats what belonged to Laban. But at least he was payin' Laban tit for tat what that old man had did to him all them years. But when Laban's boys told him what Jacob had did, he taken off after him. Don't know what he planned to do to Jacob, but plenty probly.

"That Jacob was a slick talker, though, and when Laban caught up with him, he managed to sweet-talk him and make peace.

"That dint end Jacob's troubles, though. Not by a

long shot. He had a more serious problem ahead. Remember how years before Jacob had done his twin brother, Esau, dirty, awful dirty? Him and Rebekah, they mama—a sly old girl herself—had got togather and tricked Isaac into giving Jacob the blessing meant for Esau. Old Isaac was almost blind and thought he was blessin' Esau when hit was Jacob. Esau was left out in the cold. When Esau found out about it, he said he was gonna kill Jacob. To keep down a killin', Rebekah told Jacob to scat over to the land where her brother Laban lived. But Esau, now, he never forgot, hit stayed in his craw.

"Now Jacob after all them years was headed back home to Isaac. But, after settlin' up with Laban he heerd from messengers that Esau was comin' to meet him with four hundred men.

"Esau wasn't like Laban. He was a good man—not smart as Jacob—but he never had done nothin' to hurt Jacob, and Jacob had did him as lowdown stinkin' dirty a trick as a man can do to another, just stole Esau's inheritance. His own twin brother! And now the next day was gonna be payday for Jacob.

"Jacob put his wives and childern on one side of a creek for protection, and he went off all to hisself on t'other side. That night he was all alone.

"Well, not quite. Remember what I'm about to tell you, Hershell?"

Hit come back to me. "I remember Mama readin'

about some man or a angel showin' up and rasslin' with him. Went on all night. I remember this 'cause he renched Jacob's leg out of place."

"He shore did. Now, why would the Lord on *this* night send a angel down to rassle with him? Jacob had plenty on his mind asides some rasslin' match."

"I ain't got no idear. But I s'pose you kin tell me."

"That was the Conscience Angel, Hershell."

"The what!"

"Conscience Angel. Jacob's the first human in the Bible who warn't sorry just because he was caught and gonna have to pay the piper. He was sorry because he knowed he'd been lowdown sorry. That angel larned Jacob shame. Shame, Hershell, shame.

"Somethin' else, that ain't quite all."

He straightened up his specs and swallowed. "Now us humans might, but just because a man has been low-down stinkin' sorry don't mean the Lord gives up on him. Not by a long shot. That's somethin' else Jacob larned that night. Them's the answers to this here 'riddle' you call hit."

I hope you got the point now. Maybe you see why I knowed then to keep some space between us.

But neither me or Aunt Josie ever taken him too serious. We'd came a long ways getting used to him, Josie long since larning there was mighty little hard work she was gonna get out of him. And on his religion, just let him be.

SEVEN

By and by, him and Aunt Josie got theyselves a family, two chaps, Jim Hugh and Aron. Them two as babies larned me all about what I have heard some folks call the thrush, but we always called the thrash. First off hit was Jim Hugh, little mouth all blistered out inside. Bawling his head off and keeping us up at night. No matter how long you taken him up and walked holding him, still couldn't quiet him.

They's two sure-fire cures for the thrash. The best one's to have a man what never seen his papa blow in the baby's mouth.

Josie and me both knowed Isom Boatright. They said he never had saw his daddy, and was sent for all the time to blow in babies' mouths what had the thrash. He didn't live far from our folks, but the old man charged $1.50. Same time we didn't know nobody else, and finally Jim Hugh got so bad off Josie wrote Paw, and Mr. Isom he come over.

With Jim Hugh squalling, Old Man Isom he just picked him up and gently blowed in his mouth. In less'n a minute off Jim Hugh went to sleep.

That still didn't keep Josie from asking when she went for her purse, "Mr. Isom, you don't think a dollar and a half is a might steep for no more'n you done?"

"Don't charge no more'n a doctor for his house calls, Miss Josie."

By the by, there was another thing Mr. Isom could do. He could call the name of everbody he'd ever knowed. His whole life. Over at the county seat some stranger would come up, introduce hisself, and give Mr. Isom his name. Then he'd give Mr. Isom two bits and off he'd start: "Me-Maw—brother Joe—sister Mary Agnes—sister Myrtle—Uncle John, Aunt Mary Sue—Preacher Josh Hartley—first cousin Hassle Simpson, first cousin Minnie Stokes," naming first off all his family and kinfolk, and then on and on singsong for maybe half a hour, a hundred at least or more names. Until finally he'd name the stranger, and then he'd quit.

But when Aron come along and taken the thrash Mr. Isom had done died. So we had to use the other cure.

What we done was heated the kettle till the water come to a boil. Then went out in the backyard and picked up five or six chicken droppings. We taken the white all off of them (be sure you don't get nothing but the white part—hit don't take much). Josie put them droppings in a glass of hot water and stirred a tea.

She taken a taste, swished hit around in her mouth. Then she handed me the spoon. "Hershell, see if you think hit's strong enough."

"Ain't no need, Josie. I can tell hit's plenty strong."

She taken Aron up and give him a tablespoon, and then dosed him three times a day, first thing in the morning, at dinner time, and just after dark. In a couple of days, not over three or four, his mouth was pink and smooth, no sign of breaking out. No more thrash, no more squalling.

Them two was rounders as kids. "Got my all-day sucker, Hershell?" was the first thing they'd holler when they seen me down the road coming home from the store. They knowed ever time I went I was gonna bring 'em back a penny sucker apiece; cherry, lemon, strawberry, grape, one of them flavors.

Josie'd make Abe Lincoln holler squeezing that penny. We always got our flour in forty-eight-pound bags, Pillsbury or Magnolia. She made me and the kids' drawers out of them sacks.

We washed with our own homemade soap, none of that store-bought Octagon for us. We swept up the ashes from our fireplaces and kitchen stove and emptied into our ash barrel until hit was full. Hit had a hole in the side near the bottom, and we'd put a dipper or two of water in the barrel from time to time what would leech through them ashes, and the lye'd drain out the hole into a trough. Then you mix the lye with red-hot grease—Josie knowed just how to mix hit—stir hit and let hit cool. Cut hit up, and that was our soap. Just that easy. You wash your hair with that soap, you never did need to worry about no dandruff.

Didn't matter if hit was freezing cold winter or not, Josie seen to hit the kids got their bath ever Saturday. Beginning that morning she loaded all the kettles and pans of water she could put on the cook stove, filled them with water, heated to scalding hot. We brung two washtubs in from outside, and emptied buckets of well water in them to halfways or more full and poured hot water into the tubs so as to warm hit. One tub for washing, t'other for rinching. Hit's natural for a kid not to want no bath. Ever time they'd beg her leave 'em be just like they was, but they was wasting their breath. First off, and till they got big enough to do it theirselves, Josie'd soap and scrub them fussing and hollering, then rinch them off, and me or Uncle May'd tote the tubs out back to empty. And, after the kids, me, then Uncle May'd go through the same rigamarole. Josie'd take hers last. Hit was some job, but we was all clean for church the next day.

And church was where we'd be. Church was where Josie and the kids was gonna be ever Sunday, rain, shine, thunder, lightning, or snow. Josie evermore believed in ever preacher. When the church doors opened they'd be there and when they left the doors'd be closing. She and my mama was both like that. Once a man received the "call" to preach, he was being directed by the Holy Ghost, Holy Spirit, a mysterious power, and everthing he said and did was gospel. They might not understand hit, but they believed hit. A preacher couldn't do no wrong. Course them two wasn't no different from most nearly ever woman I knowed and growed up with.

Josie being that way was the reason I knowed she never fussed at Uncle May. I knowed Uncle May having all them religious pamphlets coming through the mail and cluttering the house, listening to some preacher on the radio ever day and night, and never talking about nothing else but his ideas of the Holy Scriptures was bound to have kept her wore out. She just taken hit.

Mondays was washday. Late on Sunday first me, and later one of the kids, would put pine knots around the washpot ready to set afire, and before daylight on Monday go out and fill the pot and light the fire so as to get the water boiling. We always kept three number-two washtubs on the bench by the pot. Hit taken Josie a full day day boiling and stirring, and then scrubbing them clothes on a scrub board, then beating them and then rinching them out in tubfuls of water. Irons was heated at the fireplace or stove, and she done her ironing that night. We'd all done gone to bed before she was through.

To make a long story short, like I done said, Josie and me in them few years had made a first-class little farm out of them 121 acres, 'specially for Flatwoods. And I just kind of stayed on.

Times passed and Jim Hugh and Aron growed regular—Mooneyhams more than Yancys, I'm proud to say—neither one of them minding hard work. Me'n Josie could pick 125–135 pounds of cotton a day apiece, and them boys as chaps got to where they'd get up to 35 or 40. Uncle May was good if he got 25.

EIGHT

Then there was that morning when Jim Hugh was a little kid and come running in the house, saying, "Bully ain't here!"

"Have you looked in all the stalls in the barn, and all down in the paster?"

"He ain't nowheres, Hershell."

Bully was a pure-blooded, brown-spotted yearling Jim Hugh'd raised. He taken a shine to him from the first day he was dropped, seen he got the best hay all winter, corn-fed him. Bully was like a pet dog following him around. He curried and petted him, would of took Bully to bed with him if he could of. Josie figured when Jim Hugh got old enough she'd let him put Bully in a 4-H contest.

I stepped out in the barn lot with Jim Hugh. No

Bully. Looked all over the pasture. No Bully. I taken the path down to the far side of the pasture. There was a loose fence post and bobwire was down. I seen somebody's foot and calf tracks on out to the road.

"Jim Hugh, Bully's been stole."

He busted out crying. Ever farmer despises a cow thief. When I got back to the house I told Josie, "We goner catch that thief's last thing I do," and some more words, too.

I got a holt of Walter Catledge, our constable, pronto, and he drove over. He had one of them open four-door Essexes like they used to make, and always had that big badge pinned on outside of his shirt. Him, Uncle May, and me went down and I showed him where Bully was took off.

When he seen the tracks he bent way over, walked from the fence out to the road, back and forth, looking at them. Then he got down on his knees looking at them.

"Mr. Yancy, I ain't got no more use for a cow thief than you folks have," Mr. Walter said. "They's too much of this cow stealin' goin' on. Too damn much. Ever one them bastards belongs in the pen—onliest way you're goner stop this."

We come back to the house.

"But we goner git *this un*. He left too good a tracks," Mr. Walter told us, and drove off.

I got madder and madder. A cow thief's lower down than a snake's belly, and one what'd take a kid's pet calf wasn't worth killing. I was wishing I just could of –saw him when he done hit.

Hit wasn't over two or three days when Mr. Walter come back. "Think I got your thief," he told me. "Come go with me."

"Great, Mr. Walter!" I couldn't hardly wait.

I hopped in his car, and me and him drove a mile or so to the old Swanson place. He turned off on a field road. We went through some sweetgum woods. I felt uneasy when we was going over a old rickety bridge crossing a ditch. "Ain't nobody farmin' this land," he said when he stopped the car. "Git out."

We got out and he taken me off the trail to a bare spot. "Look there."

There was what was left of Bully. He'd been skinned and butchered by somebody shore didn't know much about dressing a cow. Some of hits guts still there in him, and one of his legs hadn't even been skint, meat still in the hide. I seen the little old notch in hits right ear, and that brown spot on hits neck about the size of a cantaloupe. Hit was Bully, all right. Probly took whoever done hit a while to kill him. I was getting red-hot madder by the minute.

"This your yeahlin'?"

"You damn right. Yep, that's him."

"You shore now, Mooneyham?"

"Yep, that's Jim Hugh's calf."

"Be real shore now. I need to know that. Ain't got no case unlessen you absolutely shore he's your'n."

"Ain't no doubt. None atall. That's our'n, like I told you."

"Looky here at these tracks. They just like them at your fence. I figger the thief didn't have no heel on his left shoe, and a big hole in the bottom of t'other."

"Where's that lowdown sonabitch?"

"Come on."

We got back in the car and he drove just a little ways around a crook in the road. Out in the middle of a growed-up field was what was left of a sharecropper's house. Hit never had saw no paint brush and was leaning over against a pin oak. Wasn't no winders nor sashes, just open holes where winders oughta been. Didn't have no door, just a opening where a door had been. A well was out front, but I seen hit was all filled in.

We got out. Mr. Walter walked up to the front. "Anybody here?"

Nobody answered. "I say, anybody here?"

A woman come out, hair all matted like a straw pile, thin as a scarecrow. Her dress was so dirty I couldn't of even guessed what color hit was. A baby girl grabbing a hold of her mama's dress stuck her head round from behind the woman, her big eyes staring up at us.

"What you want?"

"Where's your old man?"

"In jail. You orter know."

"Who's your husband, lady?"

"Hubert Sedberry."

Mr. Walter said that was right, he knowed it,

"caught him makin' moonshine." Then Mr. Walter turned to me. "Kelsie Dinsmore run him off last year when he was too lazy to make a crop."

"He sure dint make no crop! You wouldn't neither ef you had the t.b."

Then I seen another bug-eyed baby kid, not more'n two year old, running back in the house. His legs and arms was like matchsticks, his belly all swole out. His eyes looked like they about to pop out of his head. Not a stitch of nothing on him. I wondered if neither one them little chaps had ever saw a washrag.

"Well, who else livin' here?"

"My son."

"Where's he?"

"He ain't here now."

"Mind ef we look around?"

She didn't answer, he didn't give her no time to. He went on in the house, and when he done it, he said, "Mooneyham, remember she said hit was all right for us to take a look ."

Cotton wads was sticking out of holes in a bare mattress on a bed all broke down. Chairs in pieces, you couldn't of set down in any one of them.

We went in the kitchen; range didn't have no pipe. Ever shelf was bare.

There in the middle of the floor was a washtub full of fresh meat.

We taken a close look.

"Hit's beef meat, all right," Mr. Walter said.

"Yessir, hit ain't pork for shore."

"Where's your boy?"

"I done told you he ain't here."

"Well, lady, we'll just set and wait a spell."

Then, "I need a drink of water," Mr. Walter told the lady, and started towards the well out front.

"Hit's dry and filled in," she said. "My son hauls water from the ditch down there where you all come in. Ain't no water here at the house."

Then we seen a boy come around the bend towards us. When he seen the car he turned around and started back.

Mr. Walter run out and hollered, "Wait!"

Boy stopped.

"Come here, boy!"

We stepped out in front of the house. The boy come up. He had a lard bucket in one hand and a sack in t'other. He looked to be fourteen or fifteen year old. His skin was taller yellow.

"Les see what you got there, boy."

The boy opened the bucket. There was about two or three inches of lard in the bottom.

"What's in the sack?"

The sack had maybe a pound of cornmeal.

"What's your name, boy?"

"Howard Sedberry." I seen his teeth was black and rotted.

"Well, Howard, where'd you git that meat back there in the house?"

He looked at his mama standing in the doorway.

"From a calf I raised."

"Don't lie to me, boy! I know where that meat come from."

"I raised hit, I tell yer!"

"Like hell you did! Lift up that left foot, boy!"

He done that.

"Now the right un."

He done that, too.

I looked, too. His left shoe didn't have no heel, and there was a big hole in his right one.

"Them was his tracks, all right," Mr. Walter said. "Take off them shoes, boy."

He done that and Mr. Walter reached and taken them. Then he put them on the front seat of his car.

"Boy, you done stole Mr. Yancy's kid's pet yeahlin'. I'm takin' you in."

The boy went to trembling, taken a snarling look made me think of a coon or fox when you catch him with his leg caught in the trap. Cain't run, hunkering and shivering, would fight if'n hit could.

The woman walked out. "Who's goner feed us? How we goner eat? You done took my husband and now you takin' my boy!"

"I ain't runnin' no grocer store, lady!" Mr. Walter hollered back. Then he said something to hisself. Sounded like: "Damn trash. Sorrier'n niggers."

"Mooneyham, you git in back. Git on that front seat, boy!"

The boy balked. "Git in that car, boy, before I slap the shit out of you!"

He got on the front seat. I got in back. Mr. Walter cranked up and we started off. I was setting behind the boy.

Just as we crossed the old bridge I seen a louse come out from the boy's hair crawling down his neck. Then come another.

How is hit that all of a sudden hit can come about that something you always knowed was so you ain't so shore of now? Then I remembered Paw: "A Flat-woodser'll steal before he'll beg."

"Mr. Walter," I said. "I ain't for shore that was our calf."

He hollered back, "What you say, Mooneyham?"

"I said, 'I ain't for shore that was our calf."

He stopped the car, turned around to me: "Well, you damn shore was shore about a hour ago."

"Yessir, but I been studyin'. That un we seen had a nick in hits right ear and a brown spot on hits neck about the size of a cantaloupe. Hit ain't ours. Hit just ain't ours, Mr. Walter."

He reached down, handed the boy his shoes: "Get your ass out of here."

Mr. Walter didn't ask me to get on the front seat. Never said a word all the way back. He stopped in front of our house. I got out.

"Mooneyham, ef you ever happen to have any more stole cows, don't bother about callin' me." He shifted his old Essex in low gear hard enough to break the lever, and gunned off.

"Well?" Josie asked me after I'd walked in the house and not said nothing.

"Hit wadn't Bully," I told her.

I just wasn't up to explaining then, or now neither for that matter.

NINE

Then hard times sure enough hit everwheres, as you know. And in 19 and 30 we didn't get no rain and almost didn't make no crop. On top of that we couldn't get nothing for what little we had growed. Cotton down to a nickel a pound. Land sold for trust deed debts. Over a third of the land in the county sold for their land taxes farm folks just couldn't pay.

If you was over at the county seat when a freight train come in, you shore to see a dozen or more men pile off and scatter through town, going to back doors and asking the lady of the house to do some yard work, chopping wood, cutting weeds with a swing blade, shoving a lawn mower, anything just for something to eat.

"Hoover wagons" a plenty. Them was wagons the

farmers had took the wagon wheels off and put on car wheels with tires on.

Then everbody sure enough went to eating rabbits, called them "Hoover steaks."

We didn't take our shoes to the repair shop for half soles them days. We'd buy rubber soles at Morgan and Lindsey's for twenty-five cents a pair, and heel taps, cut the pieces to fit, and then glue them onto the bottoms of the shoe and tack on taps. Least we had shoes. There was white kids I seen walking by our house barefooted in November and later even.

Halls Siding's school is grade one through six, Miss Sara Holliday their teacher. All the children taken their dinners to school in paper sacks. Jim Hugh come home one day and told Josie, "Mama, when Lorene Chaney opened her dinner sack today, wadn't nothin' in hit but a handful of plain, biled rice." Then he told her, "And yesteday Odie Chaney brung a sack of hickry nuts for his dinner. Busted them on bricks."

The next day I finished up early straightening fence posts and stapling on bobwire down in the pasture. When I got back to the house Josie was in the kitchen. She was slicing off a hunk of fatback, had a bucket of molasses, a sack of cornmeal, and sweet taters piled out on the table. She'd started putting hit in a croker sack when she seen me.

"Hershell, saddle one of the mules. I'm goner ride over and visit Ora Chaney."

TEN

Jim Hugh shook me awake on a hot July morning in 19 and 32: "Uncle Hershell, Mama's sick."

I went to her and Uncle May's bedroom. Josie was in her nightgown stretched across the bed. "I'm burnin' up!" When I put my hand on her forehead, I knowed she had one sure-enough fever. Uncle May standing there doing nothing.

I run out to the barn lot, throwed a bridle on a mule and taken off to the phone over at Alford's Store. I rang and told the lady Paw's number. Thank the Lord wasn't nobody else on the party line.

"Papa, Aunt Josie's bad sick. We need a doctor."

Josie was talking out her head when I got back to the house. I thought that doctor never was goner come.

Papa brung Dr. Sid. He come in Josie's room, taken

a look at her. He reached around, pulled a chair up aside the bed and taken a seat. He leant over Josie, pulled her eyelids wide and looked at her eyeballs. Then he taken a thermometer out his bag, stuck hit in her mouth, and pulled his watch out and looked at hit while holding her wrist. Set there a bit, pulled out the thermometer and taken a look.

"One hunerd and four," he said. "Git me some scissors."

Uncle May didn't know where they was at. Jim Hugh said, "I know where," and run over and got them out the top drawer of the chifforobe.

"Mayfield, put a towel under her." We done that. Dr. Sid whacked all Josie's hair off close to her head. He lifted her, motioned us to take the towel out, and laid her back down.

"Now go get me a fresh pan of water out of the well and a wash rag."

Uncle May done that.

"Tolbert (that was my Paw's name), Mayfield, Miss Josie has the typhoid."

Hit was a thunderbolt. None of us said nothing.

"Jest like I'm showin' you, Mayfield, you keep the water cool's you kin, fresh out of the well, and bathe her face, neck, arms, under her armpits, up and down her legs, and up between her legs. Don't scrub, jest gently keep her cool as you can with a wet rag all day, all night."

He taken a bottle of pills and a bottle of medicine out of his bag. "See that she takes one these pills and a teaspoon of this medicine ever four hours. You goner need a refill when they run out. I'll tell Mr. Tabb at the drugstore to be expectin' you."

He taken off his specs, rubbed his hand over his eyes, and put the specs back on. "She's goner have a bloody flux, Mayfield. You're goner have to keep a fire under that washpot, water ready to bile all time. Her gowns and sheets got to be sterlized in biling water and washed. Changed at least onct ever day. They goner want to come in, but you keep the kids out of this room—I mean stay out. And you or whoever else tends her wash your hands—use strong lye soap—after ever time you handle her. Don't go nowheres until you've washed your hands. And she don't need no outside compny. She's goner keep that fever. You got at least twelve to fourteen days ahead of you givin this medicine and keepin' her cool and comfortable as you can."

Paw stayed.

"Mayfield, you, me, and Hershell's the ones got to see after her. We're in for a spell. Wouldn't you figure we better do hit in shifts?"

"Whatever you think, Mr. Tolbert."

"I'd say about four hours each. None of us can do hit all."

From that first shift I knowed I was at the bedside of somebody mighty sick. Hit ain't no good feeling. Josie moaned and thrashed. Her eyes walled, and she was hot to tetch. Her skin got so yellow made her teeth look like chalk. The whites of her eyeballs yellow, too. And that's the way she stayed, thrashing, moaning, ever now and then trying to raise herself up and crying out, saying words what made no sense. I went to the well ever half hour, sunk the bucket deep so as to get the coolest water. Squeezed the rag, and laid or else rubbed hit gently on her forehead, face, arms and armpits, up and down and between her legs. Fanned her. Cleaned her. She might's well been nekkid in that gown. Right at first I was skittish, Josie being a woman and all that. But that didn't last. I couldn't pay no mind I was seeing parts of her no man except a husband s'posed to see. Somebody that sick ain't no man and ain't no woman, but a pore body in terrible shape, and all you thinking about is what you can do to make her less miserable.

The room taken on a stench. We all got used to hit. Had to. Hit come to mind how embarrassed Josie'd been if she knowed how near nekkid she was and what she was doing to them sheets.

In a couple of days Paw said, "We need a woman," and went and brung my sister to help. First time she went in Josie's room she run outside and vomited.

Josie'd shiver with a rigor, and we'd cover her. Then she'd get hot, thrash and kick her cover off. Always uneasy.

Then—I lost count—Josie got weaker by the day. You'd walk in her room and you'd hear gasping and deep drawing of her breath. She was too weak to rise up, or moan, even. On my shift I started to reading the Book of Job. Mama said he trusted the Lord. I needed to.

And one of them last nights when I went in her room she was quiet, laying flat on the bed. Only sound was the Westclock, "tock tock tock tock tock tock." Fireplace was all cleaned out, no ashes, nothing but the two angle irons in hit. Uncle May's pamphlets was piled loose on the floor aside a chair. On the mantle, stuck in the side of the mirror was two Kodak pictures of Josie, Uncle May, Jim Hugh, and Aron what a cousin of ours taken. The light from the lamps was making shadows on the walls and ceiling. Crazy like, I begun wondering if ghosts wasn't in the room.

I don't think Josie even knowed when I taken one of her hands and looked at hit. Her fingers long and slender. How had they done so much work? Her breathing was long. If I had thought she knowed what I was saying I couldn't of said hit. "Josie, don't you die on us. Other than Mama you're the sweetest thing I ever knowed."

Just after daylight Paw was out on the porch. He was stretching hisself and getting in a smoke before taking his turn.

"Paw, Josie ain't goner die, is she?"

He didn't say nothing.

"She's goner make hit, ain't she, Papa?"

He looked away. When he turned back his eyes had a soft, kind of "please don't ask me" look. "Ef anybody can, son, Josie will."

I had done lost count of the time. Maybe hit was the next day, maybe later, don't know. But late in the evening Dr. Sid drove back.

"Hit's gettin' time for that fever to break ef'n hit's goner."

Hot as hit was, Dr. Sid had on his suit, necktie, and

shirt with collar buttoned up. He pulled up a chair aside Josie's bed, set down, and taken her pulse and temperature. "One hunerd and three." He set there aside her bed till dark, then told Uncle May to light another lamp and bring hit in. "I need to keep a good look." Ever few minutes he'd tell one of us to bring him a fresh pan of water, and then tell us to bathe her.

I'd guess about ten that night Dr. Sid, still setting there, taken Josie's temperature again. Sweat was on his forehead. He rubbed his chin, shook his head. "Still a hunerd and three."

"Dr. Sid?"

Don't think he heard him.

"Dr. Sid?"

"Yes, Mayfield?"

"I got a bad itchin' in my crotch. You got somethin' you can gimme for hit?"

"You what?"

"I said I got me a rash or somethin' twixt my legs way on up what shore itches. I was wonderin' what you might have for hit."

"I expect I do, Mayfield."

Dr. Sid taken his knife out, made a toothpick out of a match. He never asked for nothing, not even a drink of water. Setting in that straight chair, just watching Josie, saying nothing. Ever now and then his mouth'd take a little twitch.

Along about daylight Dr. Sid taken the toothpick out his mouth and motioned us over to take a look. Praise the Lord, Josie was sweating! And what sweating! Her sheets got all wet. I seen Paw come in.

Dr. Sid kept on setting there. I seen the stubble on his chin. Finally he stood up and turned to us. He straightened up his specs. "I do believe the Lord's goner let her stay with us a spell longer."

We all was all ears.

"She's still weak and goner have trouble eatin'. Start her off with a little soup or broth. Then try a soder cracker. Just a swaller or a bite or two first off. See how hit sets. She ain't over diareel, runnin' bowels. All you keep on keepin' watch real close. Miss Josie's still a mighty sick girl. She ain't all togather out the woods yet. Could backslide any time over the next three or four days. Don't mind callin' me, Tolbert, Mayfield, ef she takes a downturn."

Dr. Sid closed his satchel. Paw said, "Dr. Sid, ain't no need you leavin' till you have a bite to eat. You deserve a first-class breakfast, and you got to eat somers. Stay. Won't take but a little bit."

"Thanks, no, Tolbert. I need to get back to the house. No tellin' who's been tryin' to get me."

"Not even a cup of coffee?"

"No. Thanks, Tolbert."

"Dr. Sid?"

"Yep?" I knowed he was thinking Uncle May was about to ask something about what he done told us to do.

"Last night I was astin' ef you had somethin' for this itch I got."

"Why, yes, Mayfield. Want hit now?"

"Lordy, yes. Hit's givin' me misry."

Dr. Sid taken his satchel and walked across the hall to the parlor. Uncle May followed.

"Take off your britches, Mayfield. Les take a look."

Uncle May taken off his pants.

"Still cain't see, Mayfield. Take off your BVDs, too."

Uncle May taken off his shirt and then them BVDs, and was standing there nothing on but his socks.

I barely heard Dr. Sid muttering "liniment" and "tincture" of some kind of oil—could of been "mustard," I ain't for shore—which he squirted some drops in the bottle with the liniment, and shook hit all up.

"What's a 'tincture,' Dr. Sid?"

"Hit means puttin' in just enough, Mayfield, to get the job what you mean to do get done. Now, turn around."

Uncle May done hit.

"Spread your legs. Now bend over."

Done that.

"A little more now. That's good. I need to see. Now pull them cheeks of your butt apart. Wide."

"Like this, Doc?"

"That's fine, just right, Mayfield. We don't want to miss no place what needs hit. Hold right there."

He taken out a pencil and wrapped a wad of cotton round hit. Then he stuck hit in the bottle. Pulled hit out dripping. He begun fast swabbing all up twixt Uncle May's legs and onto his privates.

"Oh my godamighty!" Uncle May grabbed down

twixt his legs. "My good godamighty!" And leapt up like a kangaroo. Out he busted. He leapt from the porch, landed over in the yard. Just a-hopping, and running, he started in one direction, then he turned t'other way.

"Hershell! Open that gate!"

I started towards the barn lot. "Hershell! Open that damn gate!"

But there wasn't no way I could get ahead of him.

He didn't take the time to unlatch the gate. He was climbing over hit, and when his foot slipped on the second plank I heard Paw say, "He's goner smash his gonads shore'n hell!"

Over the gate he went. "Good Lord! Look, he done landed on his ass!"

Uncle May got up limping, hopping, running, and fanning hisself and hit the pasture pond full steam. He splashed on out till he was belly deep. Then he just sunk down till the water was up where nothing but his head sticking out like a big round cork floating there.

I started back to the house. Dr. Sid had his hat on, satchel in his hand. Paw walked with him out to his Buick.

When he left I asked, "Paw, was Dr. Sid sayin' somethin' to you?"

"Yep."

"What?"

"Said, 'Maybe that'll larn him.'"

Paw stayed on a short spell longer, and said he believed hit was time then for him and Sister to go.

He told me when he was leaving, "They's a lesson in what we been through, Hershell. This life's full of trouble. That's a body's lot here on this earth. The Lord helps them what helps theyselves. He expects ever-body to do what he can for his own self first. But when a body's did all he can, then he can look up to the good Lord and say, "Lord, I done done my damndest, and now hit's up to you!"

I walked back in the house to Josie's room. There she laid, thin as a scarecrow and pale as a ghost. She turned towards me, lips moving but I couldn't hear her. She motioned me to the bed. Still couldn't hear her. She crooked her finger and I leant over till my ear was right next to her mouth.

"Hershell, my head look like a porkypine?"

"Josie, that's the first thing you said in over three weeks what made a lick of sense. Naw, I'd say hit was more like a cocklebur."

For the next two days Uncle May stayed in the house. Had to.

He was wearing Aunt Josie's nightgowns, hisself.

And thank the good Lord, Josie got well, and far's I could tell was good as new.

ELEVEN

With the good Lord's help and me and Josie, somehow or t'other we shimmied through. How'd we do hit? After the first two depression years which almost done us in, we had fair-to-middling crops generally speaking. We could look to make twenty–thirty bushels of corn and half a bale of cotton an acre. We had us a sorghum patch, sorghum mill, and ever fall filled from fifty to a hundred molasses buckets, and Uncle May peddled them at four bits a gallon. I seen to hit we kept a pair of matched mules, fourteen hands high, plenty of hay, corn, and a good Jersey milk cow. We had peach, pear, and fig trees.

That ain't all. As you might already have figured from what I been trying to tell you, me and Josie have "green thumbs." Out in the barn lot all year I'd wheelbarrow the cow manure over in one pile. Then some time in December, after we'd done cleaned out the last of the turnip greens, I'd hitch up a mule and break up our garden. Then I'd cover hit all over with that manure, and go over hit with a disk or harrow. The winter rains would finish mixing hit all into the soil. Josie growed the best black-eyed and crowder peas, butterbeans, string beans and squash, roasting ears, bell peppers, tomatoes, cabbages, turnip and mustard greens and collards you'd find anywheres, bar none, and canned over forty quarts ever summer. We et turnip greens on after the first frost. A door knob'd grow sprouts in Josie's garden.

And with ever penny we could spare for sugar, we put up plum jelly and pear preserves. Ain't no trouble to have plenty of plums. They's plum thickets all over the Flatwoods, and in summer you could pick a tub full out of any of them so long as you didn't mind clawing chiggers half the night for next two or three nights.

And that ain't all, neither. We had watermelon, cantaloupe, and peanut patches, too. Sweet taters. Growed most everthing we ate. Josie raised so many Rhode Island hens you'd have to kick and shoo your way through them—all a-cackling—walking out to the barn or necessary house. Big old red rooster'd wear hisself out and just fall off trying to top 'em all. We had eggs to sell.

Josie could run down a frying-size chicken, wring his neck, put him in scalding water, pick him, gut him, cut him up, roll them pieces in flour, and have hit ready for the skillet all in thirty or forty minutes. Sundays Josie'd kill and fry two for dinner. Had fresh eggs for breakfast ever day. Killed four hogs ever year by Thanksgiving.

We never had to buy no cornmeal, neither. Onct or twict ever month Uncle May'd drive over to Mr. Sam Overby's grist mill with a bushel or two of shelled corn, and come back with a sack of meal. Mr. Overby was another of them few fellers who'd listen at Uncle May. Must of done that to keep his trade.

Mr. Overby told Uncle May, "Mr. Yancy, I didn't know a man could raise good a corn's you got here on Flatwoods land. Taken a good farmer to raise that kind of corn anywheres, but 'specially in them Flatwoods. You might orter try sellin' some for seed."

"Me and Hershell here do try to raise the best, Sam."

"Get twict as high a price for seed corn, Mr. Yancy. No way to raise good corn withouten you got good seed."

"Nope."

"Cain't get good corn from bad seed."

"Nope."

"Nothin' good ever comes from somethin' bad. Same goes for folks, too. You can put that in your pipe and smoke hit. My pap allus told me, 'Sam, watch out for the man whose daddy is a bastard.'"

"I take hit you don't believe good could ever come from evil, Sam."

"No way, Mr. Yancy. No way atall."

"That ain't what quite what the Bible teaches, Sam."

"Ain't?"

"No. Remember King David and Uriah?"

"Uriah?"

"Yep. Uriah was in King David's army. Wasn't no better or more loyal solder to David than Uriah. He couldn't a had a better friend. A tiptop man."

Mr. Overby was bent over pouring the corn in the mill. When he straightened back up, Uncle May went on: "Then one day old David looked out his winder and seen Uriah's wife nekkid over in their house takin' herself a bath. Her name was Bathsheba."

Mr. Overby looked back. "Now, I remember Uriah, Mr. Yancy."

"Yeah, and you remember David got to goin' with that woman and liked her so much he wanted her all to hisself."

"That's right. Didn't he get Uriah kilt?"

"That's exactly right. Now can you think of anythin' sorrier or more lowdown than what David done to that close friend of his, who hadn't never done him a single wrong?"

"I shore cain't!"

"Me, neither. But you know them two had a kid, Sam, and guess what his name was."

"I done forgot."

"Solomon, Sam. Solomon."

Mr. Sam taken a blank stare, and Uncle May got that look of a man who'd just won hisself a big hand of Rook.

TWELVE

I was shore bad needing a bath that day, and us being in town and thinking about hit being Thursday, I told Uncle May I might oughta get one. I sauntered over to Mr. Charley's.

"Hi, Mr. Charley! Anybody takin a bath?"

"Cain't git no bath today, Hershell."

"Cain't?"

"Nope."

"I bad need one."

"Sorry."

"I was lookin' forerd to gettin' in that tub."

He didn't say nothing.

"Line busted?"

"Naw."

"I could take hit in cold water, Mr. Charley, ef the heater's busted or broke."

"Ain't that neither."

"Where's Shine?" I hadn't saw him outside.

"He ain't here no more."

"Ain't?"

He seen I was curious.

"I run him off."

"Say you what?"

"Run him off."

"Did?"

"Yep."

"Shine been around a long time, Mr. Charley."

His mouth twitched, wrinkles come on his forehead. "Hell, Hershell, might's well tell you. Don't you never say nothin' about hit. You hear me? Don't never tell nobody. My old lady wanted some shampoo last Sunday, and I come back here for a bottle—now you be damn sure you don't say nothin' about this. I heerd somethin' back in the back soon as I come in. I went in the bathroom and that sonabitch was splashin' in the tub."

When he said that, I taken the heebie-jeebies. "Shine?"

"Hell, yes! He jumped out, grabbed his britches, tryin' to git 'em on. I snatched a mop handle and swung hit upside his head: 'What the goddamn hell you doin' in that tub?' He went hoppin' bare-assed out the back door, shirt in one hand, one leg in and one leg out his britches, sayin' he never was goner do hit again. 'You damn shore ain't! I better never see your black ass around here again, you hear me!'"

"I ain't never heerd of such, Mr. Charley."

"Onct he got outside out the reach of my mop handle, and whilst he was dancin' off, damn ef he didn't git smart alecky. 'You know, Mr. Charley, if I was goner take a bath, our shop's the best un in town.' I throwed the handle at him. 'I better never see you around this shop again! Never!' And he taken off barfooted."

"That damn sure beats all I ever heerd."

"I done filled the tub up to the brim with hot soaky water and scoured it, and rinched hit out with scalding water. Twict I done that. Then I filled hit up and put two bottles of Lysol in hit and soaked hit for two days. Done all that myself."

I recollected then how hit smelt funny when I come in.

"Hit's all cleaned out now, but I'm still goner let Hit stay clean for a spell longer before anybody uses hit."

He must of read my mind 'cause the next thing he said was, "I cain't afford no new tub."

I taken a seat in his chair. "Well, least I'll let you gimme a shave."

He put the hot wet towels on my face. "Shine was with you a long time, wasn't he, Mr. Charley?"

"Let me think." He studied. "I'd just got me a new

Model T. Was hit '24 or '25? I reclect that nigger could start that damn thing when I was plumb wore out slingin' the crank. I'd say twelve or thirteen year."

I looked down and seen loose hair scattered in piles. You never seen that with Shine. "He sure kept your shop spiffy. And I will say takin' a bath when Shine had got that tub ready was a prime joy."

"Yep."

"You've allus had a nice, clean shop. Anybody could tell that when he first walked in."

He studied and give a nod. "I never put a apron on a customer that wadn't clean. He washed them and the bath towels ever week. Combs was put in alcohol and sterlized ever night before he left. And ain't nobody never caught the barber's itch in my shop."

"Yeah, and he shore kept your floor clean. Soon's a customer got out that chair, Shine always had that broom handy sweepin' the hair all up."

I looked over at the spittoon. First time I'd ever saw hit dingy.

"Done the spittoon, too, did he?"

"Kept hit shiny as gold."

"Shine got any childern, Mr. Charley?"

"Damn if I know."

"Where'd he live?"

I was layin' back but could hear him stroppin' his razor. "One them houses down in Goose Holler quarters, somers on the second block, I think, don't know just which one. Why you ast?"

"Just curious, I reckon. Was he married?"

"Hell, boy, I never taken that nigger to raise! I think I seen him with his old lady one time. I don't know. And I don't know ef'n they was married or they still married, or ef he got any childern. Why you astin' all them questions?"

"I don't know, Mr. Charley. Just wondrin'. I know you shore goner need somebody."

"I've thought about that. Trouble, Hershell, is I done seen these other shops. They git theyselves a Shine, and he'll do fine for a month or two. Then he gits lazy, no way to depend on them, none of 'em—on that one day when you 'specially bad need him—that's the day he damn shore ain't goner show up. Cain't put no dependence in niggers. I'd ruther try keepin' this shop clean myself. Course ain't goner have no shine boy."

Hit flashed in my head just then how hit's a fact of life ain't no such thing as a white man shining somebody else's shoes.

"Many's the time I've heerd the remark they ain't no Shine in the county what can touch him makin' a pair of shoes—even old muddy ones—shine like new."

He closed his razor and put hit over on the shelf, then wiped the soap all off with hot towels, and raised the chair back up. Then he pulled a bottle of witch hazel off'n the counter, dashed his hands with hit, and rubbed my face.

I got down out the chair, reached in my pocket and felt around for a quarter, handed hit to him. He taken hit, turned and hit the twenty-five-cent lever and dropped hit in the cash register drawer. I started out the shop. He taken back his seat in his chair, and when I walked out he was setting there, staring off.

Don't know what on earth ever made me think of hit, but going back home I got to studying. A fool thought: Where did a nigger take a leak when he had to go? 'Specially some nigger woman. Shore wasn't no toilet at any filling station or the courthouse for niggers. They was a water fountain for "Coloreds" next to "Whites Only" fountain but no toilet. But that was their problem, not mine.

THIRTEEN

Over in the summer after crops was laid by, me and Josie'd take our wagon out on the place and saw and chop up eight or ten cords for firewood and stovewood, maybe make twenty or twenty-five trips hauling to the house. Like I said, Josie could handle her end of a crosscut saw good as a man. Uncle May and the boys done the stacking back at the house.

And, we could always look to take in $350–$400 year. Over around first frost in the fall of 19 and 33 Josie said we'd done took in $307.35 from five bales of cotton at seven cents a pound and molasses we'd peddled at fifteen to twenty cents a gallon bucket. Even after Roosevelt had come in as president, we ain't never been on no relief. WPA never had to "furnish" us no commodities neither. They give away cheese, also grapefruit juices which nobody never had drank before. They come in half-gallon cans. Sacks of flour, too. They kept it stored in the building what had been Shell's General Merchandise before he went broke and closed down. Roosevelt always looked after the common folks, and in 19 and 35 times got to getting a little better for everbody. Still not good, but a mite better.

Snow was growing into a man, but still they was times him and Sam helped. They'd picked some new songs, too. Mr. Simpson, who run the feed store and trafficked in cattle, goats, sheep, geese, chickens—guineas even—would take a truckload ever week to Memphis. At times he taken Snow along to help out. Snow come back telling how he'd been on Beale Street, "nothin' but niggers and Jew stores," and places, Snow said, "what had three big metal balls hanging up in the air in front of 'em where ef you got broke you could borrer money by leaving 'em your watch, pistol, or Sunday suit to hold." Called them "pawen shops." He had a song he'd heard from some piano player in one them joints. Him and Sam'd sing hit, and when we larned hit, finally me and even Josie, too, would join in:

> I'm goner moo-oo-ve way out on the outskirts of town.
> I don't want nobody whoo-oo-oo alway hangin' aroun'.

Now listen to me, baby, listen here to me:
When I have some chillern, I want 'em all look just
like me,
When we moo-oo-ve way out on the outskirts of
town.
I don't want nobody whoo-oo-oo alway hangin'
aroun'.

Now listen to me baby, we gwine git away from here
I don't want no ice man, gon git me a "Frigid-ear"
When we moo-oo-ve way out on the outskirts of
town.
I don't want nobody whoo-oo-oo alway hangin'
aroun'.

Sam told us Snow wasn't for sure just what all that song meant till one them city niggers told him what a "Frigid-ear" was: electricity ice box what made ice all on hits own.

When a man knows how to do hard manual labor, and he don't mind hit, he oughta be able to make hisself a living. Somehow. Lot of folks ain't never, and never will larn that.

FOURTEEN

But just as times was picking up a little for everbody, sure enough trouble begun for us. All this trouble what I been meaning to tell you about all along.

That's when the Healer come through in early spring.

Now any true blue Sanctified brother or sister is liable to get the "Spirit" in church. But Uncle May, strong Sanctified as he was, he wasn't like that. He done all his talking one on one. And when he was at a revival or church meeting, he would listen and he'd watch, hawkeyed like a teacher. Or justice of the peace in court, seeing that everthing was "scriptural." If hit wasn't, we'd hear from him for sure.

But now he never got juiced up hisself. The pain

never hit him far as I seen. That is, not until that time the Healer come through.

The Healer he always drove a big car like a Hudson or Buick. This year hit was a 19 and 38 black four-door Packard, brand new. With a straight-8 motor.

Also he had a closed-in van truck he used to carry a canvas tent, piano, his pulpit, wood slat seats what folded, and whatever other paraphernalia he taken around with him. Hit was one them big yellow, white, and blue striped tents, two center poles that he'd set up just off the highway out at the edge of town in Ellard's pasture. Generally he come in the fall about crop gathering time.

The Healer's one of them spare-built fellers, oily black hair, and eyes black as any you ever seen. Looked about three-quarters mean. His short, chunky wife had a head of hair color of dead sagebrush, hanging down loose and straggly from the bun on her head. She always come with him. When he was preaching she'd beat a big drum, and there was always somebody to bang the chords out on that little piano the Healer brung.

The Healer's shoulders had a hint of a stoop. He always had on a blue serge suit, sleeves coming about halfway down from his elbow, a white shirt starched stiff, and red, white, and blue tie and red galluses. Onct he got started that tie would come loose, and he'd throw that coat off and start popping them galluses. He sweated like a field hand, shirt'd get all drenched. And whenever his hair come down over his eyes, which hit done all the time, he'd sling hit back and wipe sweat off his face with a bandanna.

His wife she set a-straddle of that big drum. (You could always see the jellyroll on her stockings. Although up her legs was the last thing I'd want to look at.) Ever now and then go KER WHAM! on that drum. Make you think they could hear her fifty mile away in Grenada, even.

Well, this time, instead of fall of the year, the Healer he come through in early spring. The nights was chilly and rainy, so our county board let him have the courtroom. Our supervisors always cooperated with the ministers. A preacher always give a prayer at the beginning of ever monthly board meeting. (They needed hit.)

Hit so happened Josie was under the weather and didn't feel like going, so Uncle May taken me and the chaps.

Hit was getting about dark. As I expected, the old Model A didn't crank. Battery dead. Hit almost never did run on all four cylinders. So, we pushed her out onto the county road where the gravel was hard, and he got under the wheel. "Shev!" We done that and she popped and started. "Hop in!" Kids clumb in back, and me in front.

Riding along, looking out the car winder I got to thinking to myself: the one thing—the only thing—I liked about them Sanctified revivals: the girls I knowed would be there what I could cut my eye at.

Sanctified girls don't wear high-heel shoes. Their shoes got flat heels. Don't wear no fancy silk dresses, neither. Their dresses always cotton. Ain't got no permanent waves out of one them beauty shops. Their hair's wrapped up in a bun in back. Ain't no powder nor lipstick on their faces, neither. Not none.

Don't need none.

Yep, their hair, hit's straight, but hit glistens like off Savannah Lake in a full moon when ain't no wind blowing. They got teeth what sparkle, and their eyes twinkle like starlight when they smile. Roses blooms in their cheeks.

And they got a quick, smooth, easy gliding walk. Their starched cotton dresses smell so clean you know they been scrubbed through at least three scrubbings and hung out flapping in a breeze on a sunny day to dry out. Sanctified gals ain't fat, but ain't skinny, neither. There's a softness about 'em, but a firmness just under hit. (Like they say about Lucky Strike ready-roll cigarettes, "They round, they firm, and they *fully packed.*") They so well made I figure they'd outrun most boys in any footrace.

Ain't no girls nowheres prettier'n a Sanctified girl. Nowheres.

And when one of 'em like Dot Johnson comes swishing by, that little flush in her cheeks, you get to hoping that maybe Jesus ain't the only thing on their mind.

Them thoughts was floating in my head.

"Hershell! You hear me?"

I come to, jerked, and looked at him.

"Sir?"

"You see that dead possum we just passed?"

"Naw. I might of, but wadn't payin' no attention."

"I was just sayin', but will repeat hit again: I do believe they's more possums bein' run over by cars this year than they was last year."

I felt a warm heat when we opened the courtroom door. Courtroom was packed and men was standing around the back wall. Winders was fogged over. I didn't know nobody nowheres what would have drawed that big a crowd unlessen hit was Bilbo.

The Healer was behind the rail where all the big shots set when courts went on. Sanctified preachers from all over two counties filled the seats where the jury would have sat if court'd been going on. Seats of honor.

Somehow we got seats.

"Evenin', Miss Myrtle, Brother Doolittle, reckon some of us can squeeze in?"

"Hello, Brother Mayfield. Sure!" Miss Myrtle and her old man, three rows from the front, slipped over for me and Uncle May, and Mose Doss and his old lady moved over for the boys to set on the bench behind. Tight as Dick's hat band, but seated.

You could always pretty well count on some them town boys being at a Healer's meeting. "Cheaper'n the two bits hit takes for the pitcher show," they said, "and better, too." Smart alecks. And whilst we was getting seated I looked and there, sure enough, back on the back row I spied six or seven them town dudes.

"Oh, I know I'm country," the Healer started off. "I'm proud of hit! I was raised so far back in the country I can look at a coon's tracks and tell you what his hide'll bring in St. Louie, Missouri!"

On the drum a little bang.

Healer begun to marching, back and forth, back and forth: "I ain't been to no college. No U-nigh-versty, neither! Didn't need to. I got all the larnin' I'll ever need from THIS BOOK."

Bam!

"I have Somebody who talks to me, listens at me, hears my prayers. Tells me just what to do. Just what to say. That's all the college, all the U-NIGH-VERSTY I need. Praise the Lord! Praise Him!" Amens from the jury box.

BAM!

"And I've got somethin' to say to you sinners. A special message just for you. Listen at me: payday some day. Hear me? Oh—yeah. Pay some day. Hub-drub-a-dub."

Nodding and amening from the jury box. Humming in the courtroom.

"All you gamblers, think you're so smart. Tryin' to git out of makin' a honest livin'. Ain't you clever? Rollin' them dice when you orter be at work. And even on the Holy Sabbath when you orter be in church somers! Just look at you, ain't you dandies? Well, you listen at me.

'Cause yours truly here knows somethin about shootin' dice, hisself. And you listen, old boy—hear me? You're goner roll CRAPS.

"Ah-h-h-h, yeah. Craps is what I said. Payday some day. Hah-sah-rah-shandra.

"And you! You whisky guzzlers cain't keep your slobby ole mouth from aroun' a stinkin' whisky bottle. Sots and boozers!

"Payday some day! (Humming)

"Wives and chillern at home needin' a God-fearin' Christian daddy, and you out drunk somers. Hub-drub-a-dub. Stumblin' around drunk in one them honky-tonks! Oh-o-o-oh, I know you!

"Payday some day!" (Amens)

Them black eyes blazing.

"Oh-h-h yes, dear me and bless my soul, all you powdered women, town gals, cheeks painted so red, prissyin' around in short skirts, tryin to play High SO-Sigh-a-TEE. Settin' around some card table. Puffin' on them ready rolls. Is hit a Chestafield or a Camel, girls? Ain't you a dandy now! Ain't you a Jim Dandy!

"Payday some day!" (Shouts of "We hear you, Preacher!")

"All of you! Ever lowdown, hippercritical one of you! You're hellfire bound! Hear me, now? You're HELLFIRE BOUND!

"You sots ain't gon get no likker thare. But you ain't gon want none. What you gon want there is water. Oh, oh-h-h, bless my soul, how you're gon want water. Even if hit ain't no more'n a swaller. Just one teeny little swaller. But you goner find water is in mighty short supply there. Fact is, there won't be nairn. And you ain't gon git a drop, not one single drop! Yes-sir-ee, payday some day. Hah-sah-rah-shandra.

"Oh-h-h, and that purty little painted face of yours ain't gon do none you girls no good, neither. And you shore ain't gon want no cig-a-rette. Oh, no! Hub-drub-a-dub.

"PAYDAY SOME DAY!" Some in the congregation begun standing, amening, and waving their hands.

Right when he first started off, hit had been still and quiet in the courtroom. That all had changed. Since most of them come to be tuned up, anyways, hit wasn't no big job to do. (Fact is, I believe there's Sanctifieds what would get stirred up and go to shouting if all the preacher said was "EENIE-MEENIE MINEY MO, KETCH A NIGGER BY THE TOE, AND EF HE HOLLERS LET HIM GO.")

"But listen to me now. Listen at me. You—can—be—SAVED. Hit ain't too late."

BAM-BAM. BAM-BAM.

Amens, and "We hear you, Preacher."

Young Brother Asa Fortenberry pranced from out the jury box: "Ola-u-la-lee. Ola-u-la-lee. Velly-velly-volla-volla. Velly-velly-volla-volla. Mokki-lokkie-hottoe!"

Piano planking away, the Healer walking one side t'other, slapping his hands and singing:

Gimme that ole time religion,
Gimme that ole time religion,

Gimme that ole time religion,
Hit's good enough for me!

BANG

Hit was good for Paul and Silas,
Hit was good for Paul and Silas,
Hit was good for Paul and Silas, AND
Hit's good enough for me!

Everbody joined in repeating the chorus. On he went:

Hit will make you shout and holler,
Hit will make you run and waller,
And hit don't cost a dollar!
And hit's good ENOUGH FOR ME!

Gimme that ole time religion
Gimme that ole time religion.
Hit's good ENOUGH FOR ME!"

BAM! BANG! BANG! BAM!

Out in the courtroom old man Gilbert Thrasher skipped down front, and stiffened: "Otta-otta-otta, otta-otta. Folloh-molloh-my." And then out again. "Otta-otta-otta, otta-otta. Follohmolloh-my!"

Crowd a-standing and weaving, some a-crying. Hands all over courtroom stuck up in the air waving away.

Brother Dolphus Criddle got up out his chair in the jury box and come out in front of the rail. Dignified old man. He pastored the County Line Sanctified over on

Skuner Bottom. He had a set of false teeth didn't fit in his mouth good. "Brethren and sisters (clack-clack), what glory to be gathered here to see (clack-clack) whoms—(clack-clack)—oever choose—(clack-clack)—es (clack) to be say—(clack-clack)—saved."

He swallowed, started again. " Do you want to be s—(clack)—aved? Course (clack) you do. I want to make clear to everone here, AND ALL OVER MIS-SI—(clack-clack)—" His top plate went from out his mouth, and hit the floor. Brother Criddle reached down and plopped Hit back in his mouth, never missing a beat. "—SIPPI. We're in a new day, praise the Lord!"

The Healer started back in: "Yes, and you can be healed! If you have faith! Who'll come?"

Uncle Billy Richards was first. He always was. Still had that cancer on his face the Healer'd healed twict before. This time worser than ever.

Healer in a lather, hair a-glistening down over his face. He slung hit back. Then he put both hands on Uncle Billy's shoulders, looked straight at him and asked, "Do you believe?"

Nod.

"I say, do you believe! You got faith?"

"Yes. Yes, yes, Preacher! Yes! Praise the Lord!"

Healer rared his head back, looked straight up to the ceiling, and stared. You had to know he was looking at Somebody up there. Then he snatched Uncle Billy at front and back of his head so hard hit could of jerked a crick out of his neck, and yelled: "Heal! in the name of the FATHER and the HOLY GHOST, remove this sore. Heal! HEAL!"

Healer smiled. "How you feel now, Brother Billy?"

"Hit's already better, Preacher. Praise the Lord!"

Smile. "Go home. You'll be better tomorrer."

By then half a dozen or so was lining up. Same procedure. The Healer he'd slap them on the forehead, holler out, "HEAL! in the name of the HOLY GHOST, HEAL!" and away would go them limps, them arthuriteses, crutches, and them walking canes.

Reverend Henry Herring from east of the canal come out the jury box to the rail. Had on that yellow suit.

> *"I know I'm saved uh amen and praise the Lord uh, I-know-I'm-goin'-to-Heaven-uh-praise-the-Lord! Amen-amen-uh-He-saved-Danell-in-the-lion's-den-uh-praise-the-Lord-and-uh-He-saved-Joseph-in-Egypt-uh-amen-and-praise-the-Lord-uh, and-He-saved-Elijah,-Elisha-and-Ester-all-of-them,amen-uh-and-praise-the-Lord! And I know he's gon save me uh praise the Lord! The-wages-of-sin-is-death-uh-praise-the-Lord-amen. None of-uh-we-don't-want-that-now-do-we? Uh no sir we don't uh amen amen and uh praise the Lord. We-want-to-all-meet-uh-in-Heaven-don't-we? Praiseyou, Lord! Uh thank you, Lord! Uh-h amen-amen."*

Miss Myrtle come out into the aisle, waving and singing. Got to trembling, her eyes walled all back, and all of a sudden she swooned and fell over backwards. Landed KER-WHUMP!

Jim Hugh, he jumped out in the aisle, reached down and started to pulling her up.

Mr. Doolittle stopped him. "Just leave her be, son, right there where the Holy Ghost has slang her."

If the Healer wanted that crowd to sing, he would have 'em singing. If he wanted some shouting, that too. Crying or praying. Any ways he wanted.

And that night, don't know what hit was, but for some reason a screw in Uncle May's head turned and set him off. His head taken to jerking. He begun swaying side to side in his seat.

Some pain bound to of hit him 'cause all of a sudden up he jumped:

"Kum see, kum si, kum tolly i!"

That didn't get much attention. Then again:

"KUM SEE, KUM SI, KUM TOLLY I!"

Again:

"KUM SEE, KUM SI, KUM TOLLY I!"

He give a big hunch: "HUTCH! HUTCH! HUTCH!"

Then, "Foodie-rackie-sackie!"

When Uncle May come out with that, I heard a holler from back in the back, "I want some seafood, Mama!" Curious, I turned around and taken a look, though I figured I knowed where hit come from.

Just then Uncle May hollered again: "Foodie-rackie-sackie!" This time, just like some chorus, the whole bunch of them town dudes on the back row sung out, "Oh-h, yeah! Gimme some that *see-e-e-e* food, Mama!"

Fool never knowed he was hollering the words to a old crazy jazz song. (Me neither, till I was in Carter's Dance Hall a few Saturday nights later and heard hit on the jukebox. Heard hit so many times could give you ever word of hit. "I like lobster and oyster stew, but when I come home at night, I wants my fav'rite dish: Fish! Foodie-rackie-sackie. Gimme some seafood, Mama!")

The Healer got to nodding knowingly. They was more amens, and some "Praise be, Brother Mayfield" (even one or two from the jury box). And finally, Uncle May, he set back down.

About ten or eleven the meeting broke.

FIFTEEN

I was laying in bed just about asleep when it hit the fan:

"Shorely not!"

Silence.

"I'm a-layin' up here sick with the croup, and you come home and tell me this!"

Silence.

"I said shorely not!"

Still silence.

"Shorely, shorely not! Do you hear me, Mayfield Yancy?"

I heard some kind of mumble.

"You've *had* the call to *preach*?"

Nothing.

"Don't you know they's already more Sanctified

preachers than we know what to do with? They everwhere."

Kinda low: "I've had the call."

"We got so many preachers runnin' around now they ain't preachin' Jesus and Him crucified, hit's money and that multiplied!"

Real low again, "I've had the call. Cain't fight hit no more."

"You've had the call! You listen at me, Mayfield Yancy. I never interfered with you and your idears, even though most times nobody knows what you're talkin' about, and even though me, Hershell, and now the chillern have done your work all these years. And you know hit's so. You waggin' that tongue of your'n with some busybody over some religious pamphlet, one them things I'm pickin' up after you all the time all over the house. I have put up with all of that. But you ain't got time nair business tryin' to be a preacher, and we ain't got the time hit'll take seein' after you!"

Don't know how long they went, him telling her he'd had the call, and her trying to talk sense in his head.

Finally, silence.

Then . . . don't know why she waited so long to say hit. Maybe she was holding this Rook card as her last try. Maybe she didn't want to think about hit, herself. Anyways, finally, out hit come: "Ain't you fergittin' somethin'?

"I said ain't you fergittin' somethin'?"

"What?"

"Kato Spode."

My insides yanked.

There was quiet. Then again, slow and low: *"Kato—Spode—that's—who."*

Kato Spode.

They ain't never been no man I knowed or heard tell of like him.

Kato Spode filled a door when he walked through hit. In a whole roomful of folks he'd be the first you'd spy. Come to our county from over in Alabama years ago.

Back in them days wasn't no bonded—all likker was corn. White lightning. Sheriffs was paid off by bootleggers, and we had wide-open honky-tonks what sold wildcat likker and where they done pretty well what they pleased. Wasn't none of them wasn't tough. Daggers Hall, run by Miss Sue Dorley out in Shake-Rag, was the worsest. She was a woman but no man messed with her. Kato taken hit over from her.

There was a plumber over at the county seat back then by the name of Haze Bardwell, had a bad name. Folks was scared of him, 'cause whenever Haze'd get drunk he liked to whup up on somebody. Well, Haze was out at Daggers on a Saturday not over a week after Kato first taken over. Haze must of heard Miss Sue had done left and a new man had took over, 'cause she'd done told him to stay away and not never to come back. What we all heard later was he was calling customers "sons-a-bitches" this and "sons-a-bitches" that, and Kato told him to quiet down. Haze started mouthing off and Kato throwed him out. Haze went out in the dark. Figured he'd gone. But what he done was went and taken one them big Stillson wrenches out his tool box. Hit wasn't over a minute—Kato was still at the front door, had just turned around to go back behind the counter. Haze eased in behind him. Swung that wrench into the back of Kato's head. Customers swear they heard hit ring. Haze got in his truck and drove off.

Kato didn't come to till the next day.

"Mr. Spode," a sheriff deputy went and told him a few days later, "we heerd that Haze Bardwell damn near done you in with a Stillson wrench. We ready to take your affidavit whenever you want to make charges."

Kato was laying in bed, eyes swolled up half shut, a bandage wrapped all around the top part of his head. "That won't be necessary, Sheriff."

"Why, Mr. Spode?"

"I don't aim to make no complaint."

"Don't?"

"Nawsir, I don't."

"Hit's a wonder you wasn't killed, Mr. Spode, but if you ain't got no problem with a man sneakin' up behind you and bustin' a Stillson wrench over your head, I damn shore ain't."

Folks couldn't figure this out. Then, a month or so later Haze come up gone. Missing. He ain't never been found. His old lady finally went to the law, but to this good day ain't nobody ever saw or heard tell what happened to old Haze.

Spode had a head of hair what would break a comb's teeth going through it. But back of his head after that lick there was a wide bare spot. Years later still no hair never had growed back on it.

You knowed if you crossed Kato you'd be lucky if you didn't get no more'n a broke leg or busted arm when you sailed through a door or winder. A kick from a fresh shod mule wouldn't do you no more damage.

Onct the football team over at the state A & M college taken hit upon theyselves to pay Daggers Hall a little visit. None never went back. Said hit was worse'n playing Ole Miss.

There was a traveling drummer named Sam Rosenberg from Rice-Stix Wholesale Co. out of St. Louis driving through on his way to the county seat. He seen Daggers Hall. Hit didn't have no sign, but anybody who drunk likker atall could tell when he seen a bootleg joint. So he stopped where he might get hisself a drink or pint. Drummers always had some colored man to drive their car and load and unload their bags when they called on the town merchants. He told his colored driver to wait out in the car.

When he come back out blood was spurting out the driver's neck. The car seat was wet with blood. Blood was splashed onto the dashboard. His throat had been cut. The drummer got him to a doctor and somehow he lived, but hit did leave a swoll ring size of your finger around his throat ear to ear. Somebody told the drummer that night they didn't allow no niggers at Daggers.

Nobody knowed how many cuttings or shootings there was at Daggers. But with a dozen or more setting around, somehow nobody never seen hit. Or if they did, hit was "self-defense."

Most folks in the county didn't really worry about what went on at Daggers. They figured anybody sorry enough to go to Daggers Hall didn't deserve no better'n what they got.

Competition wasn't good for your health, neither. If another tonk opened up anywheres near Shake-Rag, first thing you know, late at night KER-BAM! Folks two to three mile around'd be woke up.

Dynamite.

Next a.m. half a building'd be done blowed away. Goodby, Bloody Bucket. So long, Hellfire Corner.

Our county finally got tired of wide-open joints, I 'spect mostly from seeing hit was only the bootleggers driving them new cars. So the people they up and elected Carl Bratton, a law-and-order sheriff. He didn't tell the folks he was gonna clean things up just to get hisself elected like most of 'em done. He meant it.

First place Bratton went after he was swore in was Daggers Hall. "Kato, you know you runnin' a wide-open honky-tonk sellin' moonshine. And you know I know hit."

"You astin' or tellin' me, Sheriff?"

"Hit don't matter. You violating the law, and I'm goner git you. One way t'other."

"Well, let's us put it this a way, Sheriff. You do your thing. I'll do mine."

"I'm goner do mine, Spode. You damn sure can count on that."

"Well, Sheriff, lemme say this: I ain't aimin' to go back to off-bearin' in a peckerwood sawmill at a dollar and a half a day. I ain't got no plans to walk behind no plow whiffin' mule farts. And Kato Spode don't never intend to scratch a broke man's ass again, neither. And you can take this anyways you wanter."

"You ain't gon make no money runnin' this joint, Kato. I can tell you that. I might catch you and I might not . But I can and I damn shore will park outside this g–d–hellhole and arrest ever customer of your'n comin' out."

And Bratton left.

Then later Bratton thought up something real smart. Back he went to Kato.

"Looka here, Kato. I got a better deal for you. I'll need me a good deputy to flush out the stills and 'shin-ers. I believe you're the man."

Kato never 'spected nothing like that. Hit's a long ways from being a bootlegger at a tonk no respectable man would be caught at to being somebody important, the second-highest lawman in the county. Old Spode seen hisself wearing that silver or gold badge, toting a forty-four, and women smiling when they seen him—"Good mornin', Sheriff Spode."

Bratton knowed what hit taken to dry up the county, and he knowed Spode.

And just that quick and easy, hit was Deputy Sheriff Kato Spode, a law-and-order man.

Almost overnight ever tonk in the county was closed. He was mister law and order. Sheriffs couldn't serve two terms together, so there was even talk that onct Bratton's term got over Spode'd be the next sheriff. When "Sheriff" Spode was walking on the sidewalk, white folks'd give way and the colored'd step out in the road.

Next come the moonshiners.

If Spode come up on a 'shiner at a still, he better not try to run. Kato'd just shoot him. "Fleein' felon," the sheriff would put in the paper.

First 'shiner done that a way nobody got bothered. "Anybody'd make that rotgut likker what's orphaned more chillern and made more widders than anything else on the face of this airth got just what he deserved," they said.

That soon changed, though, because hit become plain Spode was shooting human beings, somebody somebody knowed. Somebody with a brother or papa or uncle, or kids. They was even talk of shooting when there hadn't been nobody running.

Along about then there was a white feller and a colored man in jail waiting to be hung. Only thing left to save 'em was a pardon from the governor. The white feller's mama come ever Sunday, bringing him clean clothes, and maybe a pie, or fried chicken, something to eat. One time fresh turnip greens and cracklin' bread she'd kept warm in a sack with a brick. They'd set and pray together, and when she'd leave she always told him, "Trust in the Lord, son."

Sheriff Bratton lived in the jail, hisself, and got to where he'd let them set in his parlor room when the mama come.

The colored man's wife and three wide-eyed pickaninnies come ever Sunday, too. Sheriff let 'em stay as long as they liked.

Anyways, the sheriff got to knowing both of 'em good. Too good, you might say. Ever day when Bratton passed by his cell, the white feller, he'd ask, "Ain't by any chance heerd nothin' from the govner, have you, Sheriff?" And Sheriff Bratton'd tell him he hadn't.

Colored feller'd ask the same thing: "Cap'n, don't reckon you heerd nothin' from the govner, has you?" Sheriff'd tell him naw.

Bratton knowed hit was his job as sheriff to hang 'em, but he wasn't looking forward to hit. Not one bit. And the nearer the day come, the worser hit got.

Finally, he asked Kato, "Kato, if the govner don't act somehow—and I ain't expectin' he will—I wonder ef I might hire, pay you to pull the lever. Now mind you, I ain't orderin' you to, and I ain't astin' you to do hit for nothin'. That's my job, I'm the one's s'posed to, under the law."

"No problem, Sheriff. How about fifty dollars for the white boy, and twenty-five for the nigger?"

But the deputy days of Spode did end when Lesley Kellum was found shot dead at a still. Mr. Lesley was a kindly old man, always with a smile. He'd give a hand to families in money or other trouble, donate to whatever church that asked him, and give money to schools and the poorhouse. Everbody liked him, even though everbody also pretty well knowed he made whisky. Church folks went down to the jail and had a singing and prayer meeting with him that time he was sent off to the pen. Everbody also knowed Mr. Lesley had the jake leg and couldn't run. He had got the jake leg back in 1928 along with forty or fifty other folks in the county from Jamaica ginger shipped down on the GM&N from somers up north. Some men paralyzed worse'n others, some couldn't walk without crutches, some could barely walk stiff-legged, but nairn what wasn't left with a limp of some kind.

His killing set up one big stink.

Nobody ever admitted shooting him, but nobody doubted who done hit neither.

Bratton got rid of Spode, and Spode seen fit to leave the county.

Mr. Lesley's killing even went to the grand jury, but no true bill ever come out 'cause nobody could prove who shot him. But anyway, after Spode was gone, there was no more dead moonshiners.

Spode was gone for maybe three or four year. Everbody had done figured for good.

Then about six year ago back he blowed, a full-fledged Sanctified preacher, telling everbody that he'd "saw Jesus." And he begun the First Sanctified Church of Halls Siding.

Brother Spode packed them in ever Sunday. He magnetized the congregation. He might not of been in the Healer's class, and he wasn't up on scriptures anything like Uncle May. But the way he stood, way he looked, big wide jaws, big head, big man, power welled up out of him. And when he got going he rattled winders. It was plain you better listen at him if you wanted to stay out of hellfire and brimstone. I wondered if the church members deep down really liked him or was just plain scared of him. Maybe hit's both with the preacher. He's the one to put in a good word for you, ain't he, help you get into Glory Land? And you sure need the Lord them bad crop years, or worried sick when your kids was down in some fever. Whatever hit was, they clung to Brother Kato like iron filings on a magnet.

When this all begun, Brother Spode had got hisself over nine hundred acres of land, and nobody in the Flatwoods had a house like his. Delco lights and running water. A coal oil ice box what made homemade ice; so they said, but nobody could ever figure that out. He always drove a big car, this year a De Soto. He had also got hisself a fine herd of full-blooded Jerseys, plenty of milk hands he worked at a dollar and a quarter a day, and a fat paycheck coming in ever week from the Kraft cheese plant.

The Healer always give Brother Spode a special seat up there with him at his meetings. And, whenever the Healer left, in about a month or two you'd hear of Brother Spode buying hisself another spot of land.

In the courthouse that night Brother Kato'd sat in the jury foreman's seat.

He was our pastor, too. And the First Sanctified of Halls Siding was less'n a mile from our house.

And if anything could of made it worser, hit's what Brother Spode already had in his head about Uncle May. If Spode missed out on some of his scriptures—which wasn't no trouble for him to do—hit never come into Uncle May's head in the first place to just stay quiet. Or, least wait till some time when nobody wasn't around but him and Spode. No, Spode could count for dead sure on Uncle May coming up right after the sermon. Didn't matter who all was standing round. The more the better. Everbody would be bragging on Brother Spode and telling him what a blessing the message he'd just give was.

Then Uncle May'd chime in. "Brother Spode, you was wrong sayin' Moses taken the childern of Israel smack dab through the middle of the Red Sea; hit was across the *north* side." Or, "Brother Spode, hit was *Elijah*, not Elisha, who got took up in the burnin' chariot." Or, "Brother Spode, King David's daddy wasn't James, hit was Jessie." "Need to get yore scriptures right!"

"Seein' Mayfield Yancy out in the congashen when you preachin's worse'n settin' in a bed of fire ants," Spode told Deacon Lovelace.

First Sanctified would not have let Uncle May be janitor, even.

All this about Spode I done taken so long to write out flashed through my head in a split second soon as Josie first said his name.

"Well?" She repeated again: "Kato Spode."

Don't know if he even heard her. "I've had the call."

Then somebody blowed the lamp out.

I was milking Dolly. Hit was still dark when Josie stepped in the stall. Even in lantern light I seen her eyes was hollows.

"You hear Mayfield and me last night?"

Nod.

"Oh, Hershell, I'm so tore up. And ashamed! Didn't sleep a wink all night."

"Ashamed? For what?"

"I ain't never understood Mayfield. This mornin' he told me he has saw the New Jerusalem. I know I'm s'posed to, and I really want to, but how can I know he really is called?"

The thought which come to my mind was if the Lord did need somebody to preach, hit wasn't no thoroughbred loon. And she'd had enough Mooneyham in her last night to see hit. Now her idears of preachers had set in and she was all mixed up.

"S'pose he really is called?"

"Josie, that ain't what I'm thinkin' about. You said hit last night."

"Oh I been thinkin' about that too, Hershell. Lordy, lordy! But don't you reckon that maybe with Brother Spode bein' a preacher now, most of that meanness done leeched out of him?"

"Well, speakin' of scriptures, don't hit also say in there somers a leopard don't change hits spots? You tell me why with Sanctified churches all over the county—in some places you can thow a rock from one of 'em to another—ain't nair 'nother Sanctified church in five mile of Halls Sidin'."

She nodded 'cause she knowed that was so.

"And anybody who ain't a flat fool's got to know that preacher or no preacher, Kato Spode stirred up's meaner'n Rudolph Hillter. Sure's you standin' here your husband is gettin' hisself into somethin' me and you put togather ain't goner be able to git him out of."

"Lordy, that's what's gnawin' at me."

"Hit better be."

"Still, am I sinnin' to doubt?"

I couldn't answer that.

"Was I sinnin' tryin' to make him change his mind?"

"Well, that don't appear to be your problem. You shore didn't change hit last night, and don't look to me like you will."

"I'm goner keep prayin'."

So that's the way hit went. Aunt Josie she may have had doubts aplenty, but there was too much Sanctified in her not to respect Uncle May's "call." Not for her to understand the ways of the Almighty. So she didn't say no more. Kept her peace, kept quiet.

Of course, Josie and me could of put our foot down, told him, "Naw, this ain't the thing to do," stayed with hit and let that be hit. We didn't. Setting here now, thinking, after hit's all over, something I've saw about folks I don't understand. When you got one crazy man around you and something he wants to do gets set in his head, that's the time to keep your head. But say you got a crackpot in the family. He gets hit in his head to do something crazy, and ever lick of sense you got knows hit's crazy, damned if that nut won't get others to go along with him, ones that s'posed to have good sense. He's so damn set on his wild notion. That's the way hit was with us. Why on earth didn't we put our foot down hard, tell Uncle May, naw, you ain't gonna set up no church here? Tell him hell, naw, if we had to. But we didn't. We just didn't.

SIXTEEN

Across the road was a open pine shed, a half-way barn, cleared out of a scope of post oaks, where we kept the harrow and disks, and killed our hogs. Me'n the boys and Aunt Josie cleaned hit out, patched and nailed the roof down, and made walls out of pine slabs on all but the back side. Also some benches out of some two-by-eights we had.

This become the TRUE SANCTIFIED CHURCH.

Had plenty of room. Nobody there but us five them first weeks. Even so, ever Sunday there'd be two or three cars a-driving by slow. Ever one with a First Sanctified elder under the steering wheel. Acting like he wasn't looking. Spode making double sure he stayed cock of the walk. If anybody was around Spode in the same business he was, hit wasn't enough for Spode that he was doing fine hisself. The competition had to also be doing mighty bad.

Still, all in all, hit didn't make no sense to me—no sense atall—why any preacher, even Spode, would be the least bit worried about Uncle May. Not Uncle May. Most them Flatwooders didn't like being around him, Uncle May, anyways, preacher or not. His elders kept telling him that.

"Brother Kato, they ain't no way nobody goner pay any 'tention to that pissant Mayfield Yancy. Ain't no way," Flavius Odell told him. First Sanctified cars still kept on driving by on Sundays.

Well, we did get *some* members—I guess you could call them that—after about a month.

Rodney A. Massingill was a house-to-house salesman for J. R. Watkins & Co. products. Sold vanilla and lemon extract, liniments, salves, brushes, Mason fruit jars, scrubboards, things like that out of his 19 and 33 panel Chevy, or would order them if he didn't have what his customer wanted in stock. He was a quiet feller, what hair he had left getting gray. He was kinda pudgy and soft like, but not fat.

On a warm May Sunday up he drove up in his truck with four inmates—two women and two men—from the county poorhouse, all setting on boxes in back of his truck. Mr. Massingill said something about hearing First Sanctified's talking, and brung them county home folks to hear Uncle May. All of them either old or simple-headed, shaking with the palsy or bleary-eyed, or both. Patched and ragged clothes. But they was clean. Mrs. Wittle, who run the county home, done the best she could.

They all sat and listened at Uncle May preach, along with Josie and the boys and me. Well, now when I say, "I listened," that ain't exactly so as far as *I* was concerned.

The lady at the library, you know she asked me, too, what all did Uncle May preach about. To tell it flat out like hit is, I always have sort of put my brain in neutral when a preacher preaches, and, excepting that night at the Healer's when Uncle May got the call, never did remember much afterwards what one said. Fact is, while I always went—mainly on account of Josie—church going never was my favorite thing anyways. And, far's Uncle May's concerned, I'd shore larned my lesson with him. Now, when I had done already spent six days ever week trying not to pay no attention to him, I shore wasn't about to do different on Sunday.

Later that day I asked Aunt Josie, "Josie, who is Mr. Massingill?"

"Why, you know him, Hershell. You've saw him around for years, sellin' house to house. He's a nice man."

"I know, but never paid him no mind. Don't know nothin' about him."

"Well, he's a kind man. A good person. Always helpful to housewifes. Goes out of his way to bring them something they might need from town, even if he don't sell hit. Been at it, I guess, twenty year at least. And when Mr. Massengill garntees somethin you can depend on hit bein garnteed."

"Married?"

"No. Why you astin'?"

"Looks to me he'd a made a good husband for some woman."

"Maybe so."

Then I remembered. "Seems to me like I heerd some of them town boys call him 'Limber Rodney,' or 'Old Limber Rod,' somethin' like that. He wasn't nowheres around when they said it. Reckon why they call him that?"

She turned red. "When I was a little girl I heerd somethin' awful happened to him."

I could tell she didn't want me to ask her any more.

I did know who to ask, though.

SEVENTEEN

Old Dike, a brindle and black dog, you could tell he was part shepherd and part German police—no telling whatever else—come out from under Shine's bench outside the shop and wagged his tail. Mr. Charley seen me give him a couple pats.

I taken a seat in his chair. "Dike likes you, son," he said.

"Smart dog."

"You bet. He's got folks around here figgered out. He's well acquainted with ever dog in town, too. 'Specially the ladies. He ain't short on romancin' any of 'em. Don't cull no dog in heat."

"Likes the gals?"

"Oh, yeah. He's good stayin' right here at the shop, or huggin' around the house when I'm there, exceptin' times some dog's in heat. He knows hit ef'n she's five mile off, and then he's gone. He's liable to be gone a week, even two. I'll wonder ef he's got hisself run over by some car, or kilt. Then, back he'll come all dirty, dried mud caked on him, hungry as hell, and all chewed up from havin' to fight a half dozen different dogs over some bitch. He could have a ear half tore off."

"Look pretty rough, huh?"

"Oh, yeah. He might be sore, but least he's satisfied."

He went on. "Dogs is a lot like men, Hershell. Some are yaller, some ain't scared of no dog, and some might be skeert but still there and fight. Now take Dike. He ain't gonna hunt for no fight, and he ain't gonna pick on no dog, but he ain't goner run even though he figgers that dog's about to give him a good chewin' over. He'll even take hisself a detour comin' or goin' from the shop to miss havin' to meet up with a dog who acts like he wants to cause some trouble, and Dike ain't shore he can whup. But ef they meet up, Dike ain't goner run. They goner have a fight afore Dike tucks his tail. And lord have mercy on that dog ef Dike whups him. He'd better keep hisself away from Dike thereafter.

"You've saw these little old bobtail feist rat terrers. They'll start a racket, stir up a fight between big dogs, act like they tough. But they ain't a damn bit too proud to tuck what tail they got left and run. And when they see two big dogs fightin' they'll run circles round and around 'em. And o-h-h how they doin' some big barkin'. But they stay altogather out of the bitin' until they can see plain which dog is whuppin'. Then they jump in with the winnin' dog and and help chew up on that un what's losin' out. They's men just like them feists, Hershell. Fair weather friends. Pat you on the back on your way up, kick you in the ass on your way down."

"Yep."

"Dogs been around humans for no tellin' how many thousand years, so they a lot like us. You can larn a lot about folks just by watchin' dogs. Ever hear that pome, Hershell? "Dogs a lot like humans, too, / Huntin' somethin' to eat, or somethin' to screw, / And somebody tell 'em just what to do."

I thought then he was through. Not quite. He stopped cutting and looked out the shop winder out onto the street. "Hershell, you ever notice two dogs what never saw one another before, what they do when they meet up, first thing they do?"

"Nawsir, Mr. Lomax, cain't say I've paid that much attention."

"Well, you watch 'em. First off they be steppin' real quick and light like, tremblin and a-quiverin' around one another. Hair a-bristlin', and their tails all up and stiff."

"Now, I can say I've saw that."

"Then what's the next thing they do?"

"Cain't say, Mr. Charley."

"Why, you've saw hit, too. The next thing they do is go around and smell one another's ass."

I remembered that. Who ain't saw that?

"And then the next thing they do," Mr. Charley said, "hell, they have a big fight."

Mr. Charley stopped, put two fingers to his lips and taken aim at a spit bucket ever bit of four foot off. I always wondered why he never put that bucket no closer. He hit a ringer. "Hit looks to me like that sonabitch would know hit was goner stink afore he smelled of hit."

When I seen he was through, I finally got around to asking him what I'd been wanting to all along. "Mr. Lomax, how long you knowed Mr. Rodney Massingill? The Watkins & Company man."

"Long time."

"Seems like I heerd something happened to him bad onct."

"That was way back yonder, Hershell."

"What was hit?"

"Now, son, you know I ain't one to gossip."

I nodded big. Letting him know I knowed that. For sure.

"To make a long story short, when Rodney was a young man, probly along about your age, he had a gal friend. Hit was a long time ago. And she got knocked up."

"Oh-oh."

"She was a Tate." His scissors went to clipping fast. "Sister to Buster and Luster."

"Do them two still put on them pit bulldog fights on the old Wilkerson place just over the county line?"

"Yep, sorry to say."

"I've heerd about hit. Men git together in that big old barn, put two dogs in a ring, and bet on whichever dog they figger can whup the other. They don't let nair dog out of the ring, neither, do they? I couldn't stand to see nothin' like that."

"Naw, and ef the whupped dog ain't kilt by the other dog there in the ring, they take hit out and shoot hit."

"I couldn't stand to see nothin' like that. How can a human do that to air animal?"

"I don't know, Hershell. Hit's the worst thing I can think of doin' to a dog. They's a lot of money bet on them fights."

"Gittin' back to the Tate girl, you was sayin'—"

"Now don't you go tellin' nobody what I'm tellin'—"

"You know I ain't, Mr. Charley."

"Anyways, after hit was plain what the Tate gal's condition was, Rodney and her claimed they was in love and was goner get married. But Buster he found out. Him and Luster taken Rodney out and messed him up for life. What they done to him."

"What they do?"

Like I said wasn't nobody in the shop but us. Shine wasn't on his bench out front. Mr. Charley opened the door to the bathroom, taken a look, being shore he wasn't in there, neither. Hit was empty. (Him and Shine had done made up, Shine was back on the job.) He come out, still stared all around, like he never was quite shore wasn't nobody there but just us. Then he leant over next to my ear. "Made a geldin' out of him, that's what."

"They what?"

"That's right. Just what I said. A steer."

"Shit fire! They castorated him? He go to the law?"

"Not that anybody ever knowed, if he did. Lot of hush-hush talk, but nothin' in the open. But now old Buster, they said he bragged he'd druther have a basterd for a nephew than a sonabitch for a brother-in-law. But Rodney never said nor did nothin', far as I ever heerd."

"I heerd some boys in town onct call him 'Old Limber Rodney,' or 'Limber Rod,' somethin' like that."

"Some them smart alecks allus settin' round the courthouse give him that name, but not to his face. Now don't you tell nobody what I'm tellin' you. You know I ain't one to gossip."

I wondered what happened inside a man who'd had something like that did to him. I knowed about how different hit made a stallion, a bull, or a hog. But a man? Did his thinking change? What was a woman to him? Thinking about my Clara, and setting up real close to her on the coming Saturday and Sunday was what got me through some of my hard days.

"What happened to the Tate girl?"

"They taken her off. Over to the Delter somers,

where they say she married some man thirty year or more older'n her. Old enough to be her daddy."

"She have the kid?"

"A boy."

"Ever hear what happened to him?"

"I heerd he wound up in the state pententry at Parchman."

You've saw them folks what can skin their hair backwards and forwards and wiggle their ears. Might be all at the same time, or just their hair, or one ear at a time. Mr. Charley's one of them folks could do that.

"That Buster and Luster allus was a pair."

Setting there in his chair and seeing us two in the mirror, I seen both his ears go back.

"Them two a lot older, but ain't much differnt now. Now, son, don't you never tell nobody what I'm tellin' you."

"I ain't, Mr. Charley."

"Ain't but one person I know anywheres, Hershell, what can do a damn thing with either of 'em, and that's Brother Kato Spode."

"Kato Spode?"

"Yep. Now they listen at him. He tell either one of 'em to kiss a mule's ass, he'd ast, 'Which mule's ass you want me to kiss, Brother Spode?'"

Buster and Luster Tate both was First Sanctifieds.

EIGHTEEN

Wasn't long after that Sam Cook come to the back door one day, wanting "to see Miss Josie."

"Hello, Sam."

"Mornin', Miss Josie." He stood there shuffling his foot. "I hope you ain't goner mind me astin' you somethin'?" I could tell he didn't know whether he oughta ask her or not.

"What is hit, Sam?"

"Me and my old lady wants to hear Brother Mayfield preachin'." Then real quick he said, "We knows we'se colored, Miss Josie."

Josie studied. Then, "Why, of course, Sam! You and Dorah are welcome!"

He grinned all over. "Oh, thank you, Miss Josie! Thank you so much. I been tellin' Dorah ain't no colored preacher knows them scriptures like Mr. Brother Mayfield."

"Josie," I told her when he left, "you done played unshirted hell."

"I wasn't 'spectin nothin' like that from Sam, Hershell. I just couldn't tell him no. Not Sam Cook."

"Colored folks don't even think about goin' to no white folks' church. You know that."

She turned red, stiffened. "Well, our church doors goner be open to Sam and Dorah Cook any time they want to come, anybody don't like hit can lump hit! What differnce you think color of skin's goner make Judgment Day?"

"This ain't Judgment Day. We in Halls Sidin', Mississippi. You know coloreds and whites don't mix."

"Sam Cook knows his place. He ain't uppity. And before the eyes of Jesus he's as white as you or me. Maybe whiter!"

I didn't say no more. First time I ever seen Dorah was when she come with Sam, a two-hundred-pound colored woman all diked out in a pink dress and big hat what had artificial flowers. They always taking a bench in back.

I wasn't surprised to see more of them First Sanctifieds driving by on Sundays, taking a look to see if what they'd been told was so.

Nobody said nothing to any of us, though. Not then, anyways.

Along about that time me and Uncle May was in the wagon driving back from Harry O'Burns's blacksmith shop after having the mules shod. Across the road from Alford's Store I heard somebody holler, "Splinterback!" I turned and seen some boys run out from behind a picket fence and round back of a house. I didn't know what it was all about, but figured hit wasn't complimentary.

Larned later. Wirt Beard had a big mouth, always trying to make a joke. He got to telling that going to the True Sanctified give a man two miseries. First off was having to listen at Mayfield Yancy. And second was setting on one them benches, wasn't no way not to get splinters in your ass. So we had Halls Siding folks calling us "Splinterback Sanctifieds."

I reckon that except for being laughed at we probly would never have been no worse off.

But then Aunt Sue Woodall come into the picture.

"Miss Josie, I hear Brother Yancy has started a church."

Josie was buying quilting backing at Morgan & Lindsey's. "Yes, ma'am, he has."

"Well, I want to come hear him."

"Why, thank you, Aunt Sue. Mayfield'll be mighty pleased to hear that."

"Your husband knows scriptures better'n anybody I ever heerd."

"You mighty sweet to say that."

"My poor dear Flenoy use to come home and tell me about his talks with Brother Yancy."

Aunt Sue was on the far side of eighty. She'n her old

maid sister, Miss Una Craig, lived alone. Mr. Flenoy—her husband—had been dead for over four year. No children, but he did leave her as fine a bottomland as any in the Flatwoods. Steam shovel had dug a drainage canal splitting through the middle of it on out to the county line. A half section of prime bottom what never overflowed.

Folks knowed Aunt Sue had strange idears. And she was a talker.

Her 320 acres joined Brother Spode's. Right next to him. Don't need to tell you she was one of his favorite church members.

Anyways, she and Miss Una they come, and after three Sundays she brung the organ from her house and donated it to the True Sanctified. Both her and Miss Una could play it, and one t'other of them would pump away with all of us singing.

Then Aunt Sue up and ordered fifty hymnal books. Forty-one more'n we needed.

Aunt Sue spread the news at Alford's Store and the Halls Siding post office, about what a fine preacher Uncle May was, and how she was magnified hearing him preach. Likewise at sewing bees.

Then we had our first baptizing. Right after preaching one them Sundays, old Silas Sullivan—he was well over seventy year, been living at the poorhouse long as anybody could remember—come up to Uncle May. "Brother Mayfield, I never been baptized."

"Ain't?"

"Growin' up, Paw said wadn't no need to, shape I was in, Brother Yancy. And I shore want to be."

"Well, Brother Silas, we'll take care of that. Right now."

Him and Silas walked across the road to the pasture, and on out to the pond, the rest of us following. They waded out waist deep. Uncle May popped him down out of sight, and brung him up. His mouth was open and he was shaking his head around, wet and getting his breath.

They waded back out, both of them all grins. "Silas Sullivan," Uncle May said, "satterated, saved, and satisfied."

"What's 'satterated' mean, Papa?" Aron asked him.

"Means he been saved *Sanctified* style, son."

Silas clumb in back of the truck still drenching wet, and they driven off.

Even Josie begun getting dreamy-eyed.

Walking back to the house from the pasture, Jim Hugh asked her, "Mama, wouldn't it be nice if we had us a real church?"

"Hear that, Hershell?" She had on her yellow beads which she had wore special that day.

"Painted white and all closed in!"

"Now wouldn't it?" she answered. "And maybe a cedar pulpit, hardwood floors, and maple benches."

"And colored winders!"

"And a bell! One you can hear two mile away. How about that, Hershell?"

I heerd it, all right, but I wasn't about to get any such notions.

"Hear that, Hershell?"

"Yeah, I heerd you." I knowed then we'd lose Aunt Sue soon enough, even if the Lord hadn't done called her to meet Mr. Flenoy.

But none of this never got no chance to happen.

NINETEEN

Hit was the first Sunday in August. Brother Spode pronounced there'd be a deacons' meeting after the service.

We never knowed the whole story until after the tragedy when Thurlo Lovelace begun talking. Then hit all come out.

There was a wing on the First Sanctified for the pastor's office and the deacons' room.

"Switch on the fan, Brother Doxey." (There was a big fan with wood blades hanging down from the ceiling. The First Sanctified had done got electricity by then.)

Spode looked over at his first deacon. "All right, Brother Thalmus."

Old Thalmus Gore, hard as a bodock post, taken

over: "Reason we called this meetin' is to head off a matter. Before hit gets more serious. Hit's Mayfield Yancy."

The deacons looked knowingly at one another and at Brother Spode.

Asa Milsap: "He is causin' talk. My Callie's been hearin' Aunt Sue Woodall."

Thalmus: "We don't need nobody like him around. I ain't never had no use for him. Shore, he knows scriptures—he don't let you forgit that—but his talkin' is off-brand."

"Knowin' them scriptures is why he's dangerous," Node Magee told them.

"We shore don't need him out claimin' to be preachin' Sanctified docktern, no way." Thalmus again.

"Don't have to," one of them said.

Thurlo: "Aw, brethern, ain't we gittin' a mite stirred up about Mayfield Yancy? Ain't nobody ever went to hear him except porehouse folks and Limber Rod Massingill. And now Aunt Sue and her old maid sister."

"What about that nigger?" Asa asked.

Thurlo looked at him: "Well, what about him?"

"Don't git me wrong. I ain't one what hates niggers. Ain't got nothin' again one. So long's he keeps his place."

"I've heerd that all my life, Asa, but ain't never figgered just what somebody means when he says that. How about tellin' me what you mean by 'keepin' his place'?"

"Well—. Well. Oh, hell, you know. I mean . . . well, I don't want him ever forgittin' he's a nigger, and I'm white."

"How in the blue-eyed hell do you think he can possibly forgit somethin' that plain? Him black and you white?"

"I may not be able to explain it to suit you, and don't give a damn. But I know when a nigger's in his place, and he damn shore better know when he ain't, leastwise when he's around me."

"Hell, Thurlo," Node broke in. "I've knowed you all my life. I know you ain't no nigger lover. What you talkin' like this for?"

"Node, I happen to like Sam Cook. I know he ain't uppity."

"You know damn good and well, Thurlo, niggers ain't got no business in white folks' church."

"Don't niggers go to pitcher shows and niggers go see court goin' on, Asa?"

Node come in: "They sit in the balcony in pitcher shows and up in the roost in court. They don't set down with the white folks."

"Well, Node, they ain't no balcony nor roost in Mayfield Yancy's tabernacle. Ever one of you knows Sam Cook sets in the back, not in front with the others. What you want him to do, you and Asa? Him and his old woman climb a tree and set out on a limb?"

Then Bilbo Culpepper started in. "He ain't got no business bein' there atall. Niggers ain't got no business in a white folks' church. Tell you what that nigger needs: a damn good whuppin' and told to get his black ass out the county."

"Well, now, Bilbo," Thurlo told him, "you just made me think of somethin'. I got a well what bad needs cleanin' out, and I'll pay you damn good ef I can hire you to do it."

"What you talkin' about, Brother Thurlo? You know I don't clean no water wells."

"Why not? Good pay."

"Hell, I ain't 'bout to git down in no well. You think I'm crazy?"

"That's right, Bilbo. You ain't about to. None the rest of us neither. And what you goner do when a cat or rat falls in your well and you cain't git hit out with a bucket or rake? You ain't 'bout to catch aholt of some rope and somebody let you down twenty foot in that well hole to clean it out."

Thurlo looked at all them deacons: "Do air one of you know anybody anywheres except Sam and Snow Cook willin' to go down fifteen or twenty foot in this Flatwoods ? If you do, I'd like to know who 'tis."

If they hadn't already got the point, they did when Thurlo said, "I 'spect we all need Sam Cook a heap more'n he needs air one of us."

"Don't see no need botherin' Sam, " Thalmus come back. "He ain't the trouble. Hit's that smart aleck Mayfield Yancy."

"Thalmus, everbody knows Mayfield Yancy is tetched. So's Aunt Sue, but you can put it in your pipe and smoke it that even her'n Miss Uner'll git wore out with him. Just wait a bit."

Most of them amened and smiled then. One of them said kinda whisper-like about Mayfield not being too bad tetched to have his old lady and Hershell do all his work. Thurlo didn't pay that no 'tention.

"Just leave 'em be. Leave 'em alone and they'll come home, waggin' they tails behind 'em." (Thurlo was making a joke.) One or two nodded their heads.

Spode had set there and hadn't said nothing. He let 'em all have their say. Then he taken over: "Brethern, bad's I hate to say it, my thinkin' is the man's a false prophet. Taken it on hisself to call his church the 'True Sanctified,' but it ain't nowheres near the true Sanctified doctern. All us here now, we all know it, but little childern, widder women, and peanut-headed men, they something else. And onct you lead little childern down the wrong path, they gone. Forever."

"Amen! Amen! You right, Brother Spode!"

Doxey Watson: "Ain't nothin' worse'n a prophet what is false. Anybody knows that."

"Yep. They more dangerous, they wolves in sheep's clothin'," from Clingan.

"And we don't want no women or little childern doomed to hellfire and brimstone 'cause they taken a false path."

"Hit's blasphemy. They's evil in that man!"

"Give me and my boys five minutes and there wont be no Splinterback Sanctified," Thalmus told them.

Asa Milsap: "Yeah. We don't need no Mayfield Yancy, neither. He makes me mad lookin' at him, mad just *thinkin'* about him. Hit's our Christian duty to see that pissant don't stay in this county."

"I well understand your sentiments, Brother Milsap, and yours, Brother Thalmus."

They all looked at Spode: "I hear you all. You got good reason for everthing you sayin'. But let's slow down a bit. Few years ago I'd a been just like you. But praise the Lord I'm a differnt man now. Praise the Lord, praise the Lord. Let's study this matter as what we orter do as Christians. Let's remember the scriptures tells us not to be quick passin' jedgment."

They all knowed that was so.

"They's a way 'Revrend' Yancy can answer what's botherin' everbody, hisself."

They was swaller'n ever word.

"We may be 'spicious of him, and have ever good reason to—I ain't disputin' that—but before we go passin' final jedgment on the 'revrend,' let's let him be the one to show he's been truly called. Give him a chance to prove hit."

"Make yourself a little plainer," Thalmus said.

"Well, now, we all know this," Spode told them. "Mayfield Yancy's either one hunderd percent truly called to be a minster of the gospel like he claims, or else he's a one hunderd percent flat-out fake, a counterfeit prophet, phony as a three-dollar bill. Like bein' pregnant, they ain't no in-between. Hit's got to be one t'other."

Nothin plainer'n that. Nobody could disagree.

"But druther than us, let's let Mayfield Yancy show the world he's the genuine article. He be the one."

Spode wound up: "They's one way he can, and he can do it all by hisself."

"And how's that, Brother Kato?" They asked, but some was already beginning to get the idear.

Spode taken a look at his deacons. All he'd a had to done was blink a eye and any one of 'em would have took off to Chicago or Memphis, even, for him.

"Let's let the rev-er-end handle a snake."

First there was quiet. Then, "That's right!"

Spode: "Give him a snake and let him show if he has the Holy Ghost, or is Satan's own handiwork."

"That's what the scriptures says!"

"That's one scripture even Mayfield Yancy cain't argue whith!"

"That's Sanctified doctern, all right."

Clingan slapped his hands on his thighs and jumped up. "Boy, do I wanna see that! Mayfield a holt of a snake!"

But not everone chimed in.

You've heard the old saying that hisself a rotten apple in ever barrel. I say hisself a good apple in ever barrel full of rotten ones.

"Brother Kato?"

"Yes, Brother Lovelace?"

"This serious."

"Come out with it, Thurlo. What you wanta say?"

"Nobody knows what might happen. S'posin' he gits hisself bit?"

"Well, ain't that the very reason he's handlin' hit, to see? Our scriptures tells us a truly called preacher of the gospel need have no fear of a serpent."

"That's bull's-eye right, Thurlo," Asa told him, "we've all heerd that."

"They handle snakes in Alabamer all time. I've saw them," Spode told them.

"You've saw them handle snakes, Brother Spode?"

"Yep. Lots of times. They's places in Alabamer, Tennessee, too, where onct a year they have a week set aside, like a revival, for preachers, deacons, and them whatever wants to to handle snakes."

"What kind of snakes they handle, Brother Spode?"

"Genrally, hit's copperheads or water moccasins." But then he said he remembered, "Onct they was a preacher, name of Brother Turnipseed, what handled a rattler what had nine rattles."

"How they handle them, Brother Spode?"

"They just bring out a box with a snake, or maybe two or three in it, and the preacher or deacon retches down and pulls hit out, passes hit from one hand t'other, holds hit high up above his head for everbody to see. All the time speakin' in tongues. Then he puts hit back in the box."

"Lordamercy."

"Yep. They may be three or four handle a snake a night."

Node: "Is they times one of 'em gits bit?"

"Oh, yes. I've saw that, too."

"What happens when one gits bit?"

"They bury him."

Spode remembered, "They was one preacher what was bit who give instructions that he wanted that snake put on his casket and buried with him. And that's what they done. Stretched out straight right there on top. Dead preacher, dead snake."

"Don't know nothin' about over in Alabamer, Preacher, but this ain't Alabamer, and I ain't atall for sure we need be doin' somethin' this far out. Not on Mayfield Yancy. You don't kill a gnat with no sledge-hammer."

"Well, now, Brother Thurlo, I understand what you sayin', too. But let me tell you a little somethin', too."

"What?"

"He ain't goner git bit."

"Ain't goner git bit! How you know? Everbody been sayin' he's a fake."

Kato Spode had a hard time ever smilin', but they say he come mighty near then. "Because, Thurlo, I know Mayfield Yancy."

TWENTY

I never remember a better day starting out than the next Sunday.

Crops all laid by. At dinner Aunt Josie had tomatoes and fresh corn, butterbeans and crowder peas cooked with plenty of sowbelly, fried okra, thick slices of ham you could smell frying before you ever got in the house, red-eye ham gravy, big, hot fluffy biscuits good as rolls, and butter along with the corn bread. Then her blackberry cobbler. Not only that, the day before from over at the county seat I had brung home a fifty-pound block of ice wrapped in sawdust and papers, and hit was still big. Ice-picked big hunks and we'd drank ICE TEA. We was living.

After we'd et, all of us went out on the front porch. And we'd just set down.

For about a quarter mile in front of the house the road's straight before hit curves. On the far side of the curve's a bridge. I heard the planks on that bridge PLONKITY-PLONK! PLONKITY-PLONK! I looked and coming round the curve I seen four cars close together. First off I wondered who was dead, but no hearse. Also them cars was raising dust clouds and going so fast the johnson grass each side the ditches was bowing down. Wasn't no funeral.

After throwing rocks upside our fence, the cars almost busted into one another slamming to a stop. Rex "Catfish" Buckingham in his '34 Nash was in the lead. He had a mouth like a catfish, that's why everbody called him that. Seventeen men in all piled out them cars.

Dago run up under the house.

They'd come from church. All of 'em dressed in their Sunday clothes, from their Sunday straw hats and their dress shirts and neckties down to their brown and white or black and white two-tone low quarters.

Only one different was old Thalmus. As always, he was in scrubbed overalls with creases starched stiff enough to cut butter, striped red and white dress shirt, necktie, John B. Stetson hat and high-top oxblood Nunn and Bush shoes with a spit shine on 'em. He always wore overalls, even to church. Also he always carried a twenty-one-jewel Elgin railroad watch in his bib pocket with a solid fourteen-karat-gold chain latched into the top hole in his overalls. He never minded showing you hit was twenty-one, and not fifteen or seventeen jewels. Thalmus said a man what had a good pair of shoes and good hat on was well dressed, no matter what else he was wearing in between. Said his shoes come from the Beasley, Jones & Ragland shoe store on Main Street in Memphis, and him and Dabney Biffle and old Doc Davis was the only three men in the county what wore Nunn and Bush shoes.

Us on the porch all stood up. Their looks didn't stop Aunt Josie being polite: "You gentlemen come in! Have a seat! Jim Hugh, you and Aron go git some chairs."

"We won't be stayin', Miss Josie."

First they stood there, just shuffling their feet.

Then Asa Milsap come out first: "Mayfield Yancy, we come to talk to you."

"Yep?"

"Yep. You claim you've had the call to preach."

"Yes?"

"Well, us God-fearin' Sanctifieds don't believe you've had no call."

None of us expecting this thunderbolt. Nothing said right off. But in just a minute Uncle May come around and asked, "Ef I hadn't you think I would be?"

"No. We think you're a false prophet."

"And ain't nothin worse'n a hypocrite fake preacher, Mayfield."

"We ain't gon tolrate no false prophet puttin' stench in innocent childern's and women's heads."

Uncle May started to speak, but then even he knowed to keep his mouth shut.

"Halls Siding ain't got no place for no veneered offbrand preacher, one who ain't been called by the Spirit!"

"Ain't gon put up with nairn, neither."

Thalmus stepped up. That watch chain of his was sparkling. "The long and short of this meetin' with you, Mayfield, is this: when you was standin' round some fence post or somers babblin' to anybody fool enough to listen at you, the decent Sanctifieds didn't pay you no mind. But now you done proclaimed to the whole world, this entire county that you, YOU, been *called* to be a Sanctified preacher. Well sir, we don't believe no such thing.

"Precisely speakin', we believe you a disgrace to the Sanctified nomination. A stench."

They was getting heated up by then. "For shame!" come out of one of them, followed by hummings and amens.

Uncle May'd done got pale.

"We could do lots of things. Could—and maybe we just orter—run you out the county. You leadin' good women and decent childern to brimstone Hell. But us good Sanctifieds have met and ruther than pass *final* jedgment just yet, give you a chanct to show you ain't no hypocrite, no fake minster of the gospel."

Color come back to Uncle May, and he brightened. If there was one thing in his head he didn't have no doubt about, hit was his call. None whatsoever.

Uncle May looked at them. "Well now, brethern, I'll just be too happy to do anything needed to prove to you I am what you somehow done taken on your own selves to say I ain't. So let's hear hit."

For just a second I was about to be proud of Uncle May, but I seen their looks. Had they brung a rope?

Thalmus: "Well now, that's just fine, Mayfield. Looks like we 'bout to see eye to eye. We takin' you up on your proposition. 'Cause you see, Mayfield, we all doubtin' Thomases, and you fixin' to remove ever doubt from our heads. Ever teensy-weensy doubt."

His eyes could of lit a match. Everthing was still. Gore turned: "Bring hit out, Brother Magee."

Node Magee rose up from setting on his haunches. He went out back of his Willys. The trunk lid was not all the way down. Node reached in the trunk and taken out a wire box and toted hit through the gate.

In hit and all coiled up was a moccasin big around as my arm. Its head was a-going side to side, side to side in that box. Its tongue was flicking. It was stirred up so bad I could smell it.

Node set Hit down about three foot from the porch, right in front of Uncle May. "Ain't he a dandy, Mayfield?"

"We gon let you handle this here moccasin snake in that pine shed you got for a church. A snake, Mayfield. Yessir, then we'll all know what you air."

"Hear me now, Mayfield Yancy. Three weeks from yestedy we'll be back to witness you provin' whether you air truly called."

Asa: "Hit'll keep you good company next three weeks, Brother Mayfield!"

Catfish had been changing a flat and putting a spare tire on his Nash whilst all this was going on. He come up to the gate and taken the last shot. He taken his upper plate out his shirt pocket, stuck Hit in his mouth, and hollered, “Yeah! And Mayfield might want to git hisself a little practicin’ in the meantimes!”

All seventeen climbed back in their cars, slammed their doors, cranked up, and was gone.

“Lordy, lordy!” Josie moaned.

But Uncle May, he never seen them leave. Ever pansy and snapdragon in Aunt Josie’s flower bed was smashed flat.

He’d fell out cold as a wedge.

TWENTY-ONE

Nobody slept that night. For the next two days Uncle May was in bed talking out of his head with fevers and chills I knowed would kill him sure. Tried to talk to him, but couldn't get a word out of him. All he done was drink water and stare off somers. He drunk so much water I finally just taken the water bucket and dipper from the back porch to his room.

"Lordamercy! Lordamercy! Good lordamercy!" Aunt Josie wailed. "What on airth we gon do? What on airth?"

As we wrapped him up in blankets for his chills, and turned right around and throwed them off and mopped him with rags soaked in well water cool as we could get it for fevers, a thousand times I thought the same thing myself.

First off I knowed Uncle May'd put a double-barreled shotgun loaded with buckshot to his head and pull both triggers before he'd tetch that moccasin.

But even if somehow he would or could do such a thing. . . . and not get bit? Uncle May not get bit? Handling that snake? Then what?

There wasn't no way not to, neither. I thought of the shame of getting run out of the county. Or worser. That's something never happened to no decent person. Certainly not no *Mooneyham*. I ain't never felt such loneliness. Was there man or woman in all the Flatwoods what didn't hate and despise Uncle May?

"They ain't no way out of this mess!" Josie moaned. "They just ain't no way!"

Finally, I got some kind of fever myself. After about three or four days I woke up middle of the night, laid there sweating, and finally went out on the porch. Hit was still hot.

The sky was full of stars, some was shooting. Rolled and lit me a Dukes Mixture. Set there, and thoughts come in my head.

Maybe Uncle May ain't been called to preach. I'd always been taught, though, not to run down another man's religion. And shorely, you didn't call the hand of any man claiming he'd been called to be a minister of the gospel. That was between him and the Almighty. Wasn't hit? Just like Josie'd said.

Even though even I felt like Uncle May wasn't getting

nowheres in his church, who was I to question? This was unknown stuff, deep as the sea, too deep for me.

But s'pose they *was* right? Maybe Uncle May wasn't no Grand Leader. Yeah, even I knowed he was offbrand. But a fake? A false prophet? A product of the Devil hisself? *Uncle May?* Did he deserve what he was getting? And what right did they have to say so?

Well, I figured, maybe there was a out somers, after all.

Uncle Mayfield could just go away. That's hit! Disappear. We could say we just didn't know what happened to him. That wouldn't be good, but least we'd get shed of the problem. Maybe after a time everthing would settle. We'd strictly mind our own business. Keep quiet.

But right off I knowed better.

I remembered deserted dogs I'd saw wobbling alongside some road, their tongues hanging all out, and their backbones and ribs sticking out like they was about to punch through their skins. And me having to reckon in my head what that dog was thinking. Was his master, whoever throwed him out, gonna come back, feed him and take him back home? Ain't nothing lower down than taking a unwanted puppy out 'side some road and leaving him. To get et up with the ticks and mange and starve. Better just shoot it.

And dumping Uncle May off for good in some strange place without Josie or me where nobody knowed him would be like throwing a puppy out.

That was something I knowed wasn't going to happen.

Moreover, Uncle May might be scared crazy, but he wasn't gonna run. Big a fool as he was, like Mr. Charley's Dike, he wasn't gonna run.

Setting there, rolling and lighting cigarettes one after t'other, I begun to think about false prophets, fake preachers.

My mama used to read to us from the Good Book. She read us lots of stories, but I called to mind the ones about Jesus in the Bible doing kind and good things.

Mama said, "People down deep is good. We live in hard times, but ever human owes hit to help others. Be kind to others. When a neighbor's in trouble, you help him."

My brother asked her, "Mama, s'pose a lowdown boy is mean to you. Two thowed clods at me today. You ain't s'posed to take that, air you?"

"No, son, you ain't. But as you get older, if you try to, you'll see that ever human being has good in him, too. Look for that good. Times I know hit's hard to do. But try and be kind even to that person you believe is doin' you wrong."

"Why?"

"'Cause if you look for the good in him, he might surprise you. God made you, but He also made that boy who thowed clods at you."

Then my mama said, "This Old Book is about lots of things, but the main thing hit's about is love and kindness to your neighbor. Even if you forgit everthing else, remember this."

Hit come to my mind about grubbing day to day at man-killing labor. And all them years. How wore out I was at the end of ever day. About times I'd be plowing new ground. Hit a stump root and the plowstock bust me in the belly so hard hit'd knock my wind all out, sometimes made me want to vomit. How miserable hot our summers always was, and how my bones'd ache in freezing cold winters. I even thought about them ax handles I'd had to wipe off after some cow messed on hit. "Of all the places in this barnyard why'd she always pick a ax handle to hit on?" And busting ice on the pond in winters so's the stock could get water. I thought about making a cotton crop, how hit taken all of us with hoes keeping the grass out. I thought about Jim Hugh's and Aron's hands when we started them picking cotton, how they was blistered and bleeding till they got callused over like mine and Josie's. And about us wondering many a year if the crop would even pay our furnishing. Barely squeezing by. Always poor. All a honest man knowed was hard labor all his life. Always poor. Always dirt poor, and no ways out. I'd never got round to thinking about them things what Mama told us.

Then I got to thinking about false prophets.

Preaching from some fancy pulpit that humans was sorry, low down and no 'count and going to Hell shore wasn't what Mama had tried to larn us about the Book.

Or to hate folks. Or to be jealous of your neighbor. To believe ever other feller was out to do you in.

And I never heard my mama say one single time that Catholics, Baptists, Methodists—everbody but Sanctifieds—was hellfire bound neither. No, everbody, everbody, my mama said, was God's children.

Preaching hate and untrust. Living better'n and richer'n any of your congregation. Then hit come to me that Brother Spode wasn't preaching my kind of religion.

Maybe Uncle Mayfield wasn't what a body might think a preacher oughta be. He never done no harm to nobody. Least as far as I seen. And eventually he might even do some good.

Kato Spode and that Healer strutting and shouting. Scaring you. They never made nobody better by listening at them. Made you not trust others, even hate yourself. And they lived mighty high on the hog. Driving big cars, smoking ready-roll cigarettes theyselves same time they was telling womenfolks they was sinning to smoke! Shorely they knowed what hit was to miss a meal. Did neither one care?

Them talking about fake preachers? False prophets? What was they?

Hit come to my mind then onct way back when I was a little chap, and falling and bruising my head on a rock. Then running in the house hollering and crying, and hiding my head in Mama's apron. I remembered her picking me up, setting in a rocker, and holding me close to her as she rocked me to sleep.

Mama, now in her grave from the t.b. Oh, how I wished for her now! If she could just talk to me now! All them was thoughts what I'd never had before.

Then I went back in the house. And then I went to sleep.

TWENTY-TWO

An answer, of sorts, come to us the next morning.

"Snake's gone! That snake's gone!" Aunt Josie woke me up yelling. "That cage's turned over and snake's gone!"

"I knowed it! I knowed it!" Aron was shouting, too. "Mama, last night I seen a haint in BVDs flyin' out in the yard!"

"A haint? In *BVDs*? I'm a mind to slap you, Aron!"

"Yessum hit was, too! I ain't lyin', Mama! I was too skeert to even holler. I know hit taken that snake for sure!"

"Josie," I told her, "could of been one of them varmints been gittin' our chickens. They kill snakes, too. That's one thing good about 'em."

"How'd a varmint turn over that cage?" she asked.

Everbody (except Uncle May) walked all round the yard looking, and I raked all under the house. That moccasin wasn't nowheres around.

Went back in the house. Uncle May was setting up side of his bed. Looked like he'd just been embalmed, but at least he didn't have no signs of chills or fever. And he had his clothes on.

"That snake's gone!"

No answer from him.

"Well, I'm proud and thank the Lord for it," Aunt Josie said, "however hit got loose."

He was still looking off and not hearing us. I'd never saw him look nothing like this. "Uncle May? Uncle May! You all right?"

"The Lord works in mysterious ways, His wonders to behold."

"We know that, Mayfield Yancy. But Hershell's astin' you a question."

"Jim Hugh." Uncle May spoke soft and slow. "Jim Hugh, you and Aron git one of them lard buckets. Then I want you to go find a snake. But just be shore he's little."

"What on airth's on your mind, Mayfield Yancy?"

I knowed a lot of things was on Aunt Josie's mind, and mine too. I was thankful he wasn't going to be touching no moccasin. But he wasn't making no sense to me then, neither.

Uncle May, though, had the answer that suited him.

"I ain't made no commitment to what kind of snake I'm goner handle."

"What that you sayin'?"

"A Higher Power is drecting all you have saw or will see. Elsewise I wouldn't be handlin' any snake. That's good enough for the Lord, and hit's good enough for me. Scriptures just say 'serpent,' don't say what kind." He was right talking about some Higher Power directing him. Anybody who knowed Uncle May'd know hit'd take a Higher Power to get him to touch any snake.

But like I done told you, I never figured how the wheels turned in Uncle May's wobbly head.

Anybody with half sense would of knowed what he had set his head on was crazy as a loon. Now we was fixing to be worse'n laughed at.

Only trouble was me nor Josie hadn't any better idear. We didn't know what to do. We was at our rope's end, too.

So the boys they taken a Swift's lard bucket. And, as you'd know next day here they come running to the house. "We got one! We got one!"

Uncle May he didn't look in the bucket. "Put hit in that wire box," he told them.

"Kin we keep him, Hershell?"

"Do what your daddy says."

They opened the lid to the bucket and then the wire box, and in hit wriggled. You might not believe hit, but to me that snake was kinda pretty. Hit was about eighteen inches to two foot long. Hit had red, black, and yellow rings all running round hit. Wasn't no moccasin. For sure.

"We seen it down the end of the cotton rows, close to the slough."

"He almost got away into the water, but we got hit and put him in the bucket!"

"Didn't do nothin' but wriggle."

Them boys was proud as punch of theyselves.

The middle that night I woke up to the worsest racket I ever heard going on in Josie's and Uncle May's bedroom. Josie screaming, hollering, freaking out.

"Mayfield Yancy, do you realize what you have did to your boys and me? All me, Hershell, and your kids've labored for all these years about to be lost. Lost! Just because you won't listen at nobody. You ain't got one lick of sense!"

He musta been laying there in bed—I can see him all covered up excepting his head sticking out.

"Do you hear me, Mayfield Yancy? Damn you, do you hear me?

"I said to you, Mayfield Yancy, damn you, do you hear me?"

"Scripture don't say what kind of serpent you're s'posed to handle. The Lord is drectin' what I do."

I heard a crash sounded like metals clanging together. Next morning I seen what hit was. She'd picked up one them flatirons what always set by the fireplace and throwed hit at that head sticking out twixt the covers. Good thing she missed. Not over four inches above his head was the damndest dent in that iron bedstead.

Flatiron laying out on the floor.

TWENTY-THREE

Now I know you bound to be thinking how could anybody with good sense ever believe what Mayfield Yancy had in his head was gonna get by. He might of been crazy terrified, but shorely Hershell Mooneyham and Josie Mooneyham Yancy hadn't lost ever brain in their heads.

I don't know if I can tell you. I was in a daze, myself, trying to put off thinking about what couldn't be nothing else but a dead end. They wasn't nothing else we could think of. Then me and Josie both, I guess, just give up, just gonna let the mop flop.

Then come getting ready for the storm we knowed was coming.

First off I had to hide the box. All kinds of busybodies and First Sanctifieds'd be by to see the moccasin. Also, had to somehow or 'nother keep our snake alive.

So, I hid the box back in the far end of the corncrib. Wet hit real good, put water in a bucket lid, and kept flies, worms, and tadpoles in the water. Wanted hit to have plenty to eat.

Like I figured, the curious and the snoopers, they come.

"Naw, Uncle May ain't talkin' to nobody." And, "Naw, we ain't showin' the snake. You'll see hit when the time comes."

This went on over and over ever day. Finally I got enough. I told old snooping Peck Waldrop the next s.o.b. wanted to see that snake I was going to see how he liked hit for his necktie.

That word got around, and they stopped coming by to ask questions. Didn't stop the driving by the house slow and gaping, though.

We managed somehow to get through the week. And Uncle May, he begun to improve. Still, hit was taking everthing in him to get hisself braced to touch even that little old snake. Off in a room by hisself he'd be holding his arms out straight, praying away to the Lord to "pertect him" in handling that "dangerous reptile," just as "Danell in the lion's den" or "Jonah in the whale."

He had me scratching my head. Had the fool done fooled hisself, even, into thinking a snake that couldn't hurt nobody somehow was dangerous? And if he hadn't been fool enough to fool hisself, shorely he knowed, shorely he had enough sense to know he wasn't fooling the good Lord.

And how could a man who didn't have no more sense than to tangle with the meanest man in the state somehow be scared of a little old grass snake?

He never said nothing about wanting to look at hit.

I done most of the planning for the Big Day. I knowed we'd have to have the Model A ready to leave soon and fast. Aunt Josie'd wrote a cousin of ours, Sultan Biggers over in the Delta, that Uncle May'd be needing to come over and stay for a spell.

I knowed I'd have to be the one standing by Uncle May. I figured to put the snake in a croker sack, and dump hit on Uncle May with him holding his arms out. Then, whatever happened, at least I'd be there to scoot him pronto out back through the scope of woods. We'd get gone and nobody'd know where.

Course I knowed Uncle May leaving'd be hard on us. Gossiping. And 'specially the kids at school. But we had a farm all paid for and I could take their talk. And, maybe, just maybe, things might quiet down in a month or so.

We was satisfied his preaching days was over. That part didn't worry us none.

Then there was that dark cloud in back of my mind: Kato Spode.

So the plan was worked out almost altogether over the next few days. Rather than a sack, I got me a ten-gallon milk can. I would stand beside Uncle May, and lean the open end of the can over on his shoulder. That way the snake could come out, and I figured, or hoped, slide right on off him onto the ground. Then pronto I'd scoot Uncle May out back through the woods lot. I knowed that better be quick.

Also, about two hundred yards from the house and on the far side of the wood lot was a elderberry thicket on the side the road where I was gonna park the car. We'd head there.

Out from his pulpit I nailed in a area about fifteen foot square with a single rail so that nobody would be too close around us. Leave me and Uncle May some wiggle room.

One night the middle of that last week just Josie and me was in the kitchen finishing up washing the dishes. She'd sent Jim Hugh and Aron off outside.

"Got a letter from Sultan today. Said they had a extra room and Mayfield was welcome to stay with them as long as he pleased."

"That's good."

"Also wrote there's a fish camp on Moon Lake close by, and he can help them folks what run the camp with their boats, paddles, and stuff, sell bait. Said he could pick up a little change and help on his board."

"Fine."

"How long reckon he'll have to stay gone?"

"That I don't know, Josie."

She taken the kettle off the stove, scalded and

drenched the dishes. "Hershell, I done got to where I cain't even think!"

I taken my time drying the dishes. I knowed she needed hitting again with both barrels, but steadying at the same time. I'd already done did all kinds of long and hard thinking what that crowd was likely to do onct it seen Uncle May wasn't handling no moccasin.

I knowed hit was bound to have been pumped in the heads of them First Sanctifieds that this was a providently ordained test, with a Higher Power looking down to protect Uncle May from that moccasin only if'n he was a truly called Sanctified pastor. That crowd would be expecting to see Uncle May take a holt of that moccasin snake them deacons had brung to the house, hold hit up, move hit around in his hands and handle hit, and would hit not bite him, which hit shore was gonna do if he was a false prophet.

What they would be wanting to see was was he gonna get bit. And if'n he was bit, would he live or die? Would they see him die right there in front of them? What makes folks want to see another human get hurt bad? I didn't doubt but what plenty of them wanted to see him bit. And them First Sanctifieds called hit religion. They wasn't no different than them men watching pit bulldogs going at hit.

And I knowed wasn't none of them ever liked Uncle May, anyways. Plenty of them thought he figured he was smarter'n they was, which he probly did. That ain't no good way to make folks like you. They was bound to think they'd been cheated. And, worser, they'd think Uncle May figured they was big enough dunces not to see through what he was doing, trying to pull off. Handling a "lil ole grass snake just as though he was poisonous! How dumb does that smart ass think we air?" All that'd be going through their heads. And then that crowd was gonna get madder'n hell and wasn't no way on God's green earth to tell what they might do.

"Josie, you got to keep a holt of yourself, keep steady. I'm gonna have to git Uncle May out quick before anybody has time to think what we done."

"I know."

"You got to keep a holt of yourself, Josie, keep steady. We done gone over hit plenty, but you sure Uncle May understands, really understands this, and got hit all in his head?"

"Oh, yes. Hit has sank in. He's done got all his clothes packed. He knows he's goner have to get gone. For sure, he knows that now. Mighty well."

I taken the dishpan and throwed the water out the back door. "Somethin' else, Josie. You know I ain't goner be here when the tornader hits."

"Tornader?"

"You betcha. That crowd is goin' to be awful upset soon's hit gets through their heads what's happened. They ain't gon be nice, church-goin' folks. They gon be wantin' to lynch somebody. If they got holt of Uncle May no tellin' what'd happen."

"But you can get away? Cain't you?"

"I feel okay on that. I figure things goner be in a up-roar first off, give us a chanct to scoot. But then they goner be mad, crazy mad, and head for the house. I look for them to tear this house apart."

She started to trembling. "Go through all my house?"

"You betcha. Ever closet, above ceiling, under the house, outhouse, in the barn, out in the paster, ever-wheres. Lookin' for him. They goner ransack and tear things apart. And I ain't gon be here to stand up to them. But leastwise you and the kids ain't likely to have nothin' hurt more'n your feelins."

"How long will Mayfield have to be gone, reckon?"

"I done told you, Josie, I got no idear. Maybe two, maybe three months. No way to tell. Maybe a year even. Don't know. Let's just get through that damn day. Then we can sort things out. See where we air then. Hit will be a good long spell, no doubt about hit, but things'll finally settle down. They always do. Look our hands over when hit's quieter. You and me and the kids gon make hit. Remember we *air Mooneyhams*."

"What a nightmare all this is, Hershell! I never would have dreamt people could get so stirred up. Can you believe any such thing could happen anywheres like we got goin' on here in Halls Sidin'?"

"Nope. Never heerd of nothin' like this nowheres else. But I don't know nowheres else got anybody like Kato Spode. Or Mayfield Yancy, ehither, for that matter."

"And to think of hit! All this brought on by two men as differnt as any two men can be."

They was different all right, different from everbody else, and different from each other. But I'd done long since figured out that hit wasn't their difference, but how them two was *alike* that caused the problem. Uncle May was scared of hard work and Kato Spode he despised it. Both trying to get out of honest labor and both trying to be something they wasn't all stirred together was what had made this witches' brew. And then both come from somers else than our county.

TWENTY-FOUR

I knowed the Model A oughta have a last-minute check-up, oil change and tuning. So Friday right after dinner I taken off to Cooner's Auto Shop. Supervisor had just graded my side the road, and had a good easy drive, like riding on pavement. Cooner's got points changed along with the oil, and the car was in tip-top shape in short order. At a gas station I pumped just over nine gallons and filled the tank. Hit taken a whole dollar's worth of gas, lacking one penny.

I knowed I needed to get me a haircut and shave, too, whilst I was at it. Went to a different barber, though, where less likely I'd be asked questions, Elmo Marler's shop. Taken myself a seat.

While I was setting there waiting I seen something made me forget the haircut. One of them picture magazines, *Life*, had a story about snakes in the U. S., with pictures of them, king snakes, blue racers, moccasins, rattlers, all kinds.

Then hit showed another.

"CORAL SNAKE, THE MOST POISONOUS IN AMERICA."

I looked at that picture, the rings and so on. Hit shore *looked* like that snake in our corncrib, but I taken a little comfort when the piece also said that a lots of snakes which wasn't harmful looked like corals.

I tore them sheets out and decided to leave pronto right then.

Hit wasn't easy, but all the way to the house I kept hoping, "Hit cain't be, not that snake. Them boys handled hit okay."

I struck out to the barn.

They'd wrote in the magazine that a harmless snake that looked like a coral would have red and yellow rings, but between them there'd be some different color.

But there warn't no other color on our snake. Hit had wide red and black rings, and yellow narrow rings, just like the picture. Nothing between the red and yellow. *Life* magazine also said, and the picture showed, that hits nose was black and the head was yellow.

So was ours! Hit looked like they had took a color picture of our snake.

Jim Hugh and Aron had brung, and I'd been feeding, a one-hundred-percent, pure-bred coral snake!

I run and brung Josie out to the barn.

"That snake's pizenuss!"

She looked from picture to the snake, from snake to the picture.

"My lord! My lordamercy! Oh, my lordamercy!" Her knees come out and she withered away down in the dirt.

Quietly, I said, "Josie, I better go tell him now. The car's already set to go. Got to git him gone tonight. Sultan's?"

Gnats was flying around her face.

"Don't. No, don't."

She looked up at me. Some of her jaw teeth was missing. Wide streaks of gray in her hair, which onct had been the one pretty thing about her. Haircrack lines was running out from her mouth. Her face was the color of Flatwoods clay.

I was looking at a Josie I'd never saw before. She was a old woman at thirty-four.

"No. Don't tell him."

That absolutely blowed my mind. "Don't tell him, Josie! My lordamighty, don't tell a man he's gon be handlin' a pizenuss snake? I cain't—"

Then I seen her look. Hit wasn't hard. Hit wasn't soft. I would say kind of begging, but naw, that ain't right, neither. Hit was a "don't you understand?" look. Kind of look Paw might have give me. I don't know if she would of or could of put hit in words why she said, "No. Go ahead jest like you was. Don't. Don't say nothin'."

Her faded pink dress was thin as cheesecloth. Knuckles on her fingers was swoll out like knots on a tree. I remembered the tail ends of our washdays when I'd saw them fingers bleeding.

"No. Go ahead just like you was. Don't. Don't say nothin'."

So us two went back to the house.

Uncle May was practicing, still getting up on his nerve, holding his hands and arms straight out, and proclaiming, "Lord, *thou* knowest I'm about to handle this *pizenuss* viper. Please, Lord, guide me through this peril."

Me and Josie looked at one another. I wondered again if the fool really thought he was fooling the Lord.

Anyways, I knowed *now* the Lord was going to oblige him.

I set in to setting my mind on just what we was gonna do tomorrow, shoving everthing else out, or trying to. All this has larned me how you made up so as to try and keep thoughts you cain't stand to think of out of your head, or leastwise way back in the back.

We went through the motion of eating supper, Josie not saying nothing, and I shore didn't feel like talking none. Then, along about the tail end, danged if Uncle May didn't pipe up, "Josie, Hershell, this remind you of the Bible? Remember the Last Supper?"

Josie got up and run out of the kitchen.

I shivered. If'n that old goat had of said that yesterday hit would of hit me as being funny. Course in a mean sort of way hit still was. He just didn't know who the joke was on.

I went to bed trying my best to keep my mind set on just exactly what we'd planned all along for tomorrow. Hit was one them real hot nights, but I knowed I bad needed to get some sleep. I laid there and laid there, couldn't sleep. I got up, all sweaty wet, and set aside the bed. Then laid back down. Still couldn't sleep.

Finally I went out on the porch and set in a chair. Started rolling me a cigarette. Lit up.

Damn Mayfield Yancy! Ain't never been worth nothing. Useless as tits on a boar hog. Damn his crazy hide! He's free, white, and twenty-one, and the one what got his ass and all the rest of us in this mess. Brung hit ever bit on hisself. I didn't have nothin to do with hit. I ain't his damn pappy. Hit's his little red wagon. Let him pull hit.

Then I begun laying hit on Josie. Hellfire, I wasn't Mayfield Yancy's wife. She's the one what taken it in her head to keep quiet. Not me. I would of told him if she hadn't of stopped me. I shore would. Whatever come in her head when she seen that snake picture? I was too wore out to argue. She damn shore meant to end this game tomorrow, one way t'other. I damn shore didn't have nothing to do with this.

And damn hit all to hell, why'd I ever come to them Flatwoods, anyways? Hit all oughta stayed in white oaks. Damn near'd kill any man trying to farm hit. I oughta stayed on Pontotoc ridge. Hit's the gospel fact a man after a while gets to looking like the land he lives off of, and ain't no trouble to tell a Flatwoods farmer. Ain't no such thing as a fat one, skin's tallow and color of Flatwoods dirt, his eyes most likely are bloodshot, and he either got a hangdog or mean look—or both—'cause that Flatwoodser damn shore knows he ain't got nothing and ain't never gonna get nothing but a hard-ass time.

Damn Mayfield Yancy and damn ever peckerwood mail order preacher what ever come into our county!

All them thoughts, though, just went kersplat against a brick wall in back of my head letting me know Hershell Mooneyham, too, wasn't being the man he oughta be. Show you how near crazy I was, that "Conscience Angel" that fool had told me about come to mind. Was he around?

Still all in all I knowed somehow nothing was gonna change, and we was gonna go ahead just like we'd planned.

Setting there miserable, and rolling one cigarette after t'other, I wound up two sacks of Bull Durhams. Loneliest I ever been.

TWENTY-FIVE

I was still setting there on the porch just before daylight when Mr. Rodney drove up in his panel truck. He turned his lights out, killed the motor, and got out.

"I don't know nothin', and ain't astin' you to tell me nothin'. But tell Brother Mayfield and Miss Josie I aim to stay here at the house. All today. And all tomorrow, too, if necessary. You all jest go on about your business, whatever hit is. I'm goin' to be here."

I seen he had a double-barrel 12-gauge Winchester, full choke.

As you'd figure, folks started coming early. They brung chairs, planks, and made benches. The deacons of the First Sanctified taken charge of the crowd. I went over and told old Thalmus and Asa to keep the congregation at least ten feet back from the rail. The scope of post oaks begun just behind the shed, so I didn't have to worry about the back side. But folks was spreading all out to the front and both sides.

Hours ahead they was cars, they was flatbed trucks which had hauled folks, they was wagons alongside the road and three school buses. Some had rode on horseback and their horses was hitched to trees. Dust had done caked over cars, trees, bushes, and grass. Before hit was over that crowd must of covered three to four acres.

They was a fizz drink stand, Coca-Colas, RCs, Nehis, grapes, cream sodas, and Orange Crushes in tubs with ice in them. Dave Kyle had brung a barrel with water and chunks of ice in hit, and a half dozen gourd dippers. He planned to run for sheriff next year.

The First Sanctified's deacons had special seats in front for theyselves, but since they was looking for a moccasin to come out of the wire box, hit wasn't no trouble getting them to stay back. Also, couldn't help but notice Mike Childs had hisself a four-foot stick, and one feller had brung in a single tree off'n his wagon. Them two wasn't taking no chances.

I kept Uncle May and Josie at the house long as we could. Uncle May had hisself all dressed up, shaved and starched. What was he thinking besides being scared? About to be the main attraction at the biggest shindig ever taken place in Halls Siding. He was muttering to hisself. Praying maybe.

Josie was walking death, and I knowed she *shore enough* had been praying.

Bad as mine was, I knowed her conscience bound to be bothering her worser. What would we say to one another this time tomorrow? But I shoved all them thoughts to back of my head again.

She'n Uncle May walked together across the road to the tabernacle.

I kept feeling in my pocket being shore I had my knife. I didn't want no trouble, but if one them First Sanctifieds come after any of us before I could get away I aimed to sink hit in his belly and walk around him.

I went to the crib. That coral snake lay coiled up, not moving, them yellow, orange-red, and black rings still as you please.

I picked up the box and opened hit just above the milk can. I leant the box over steep and real easy shaken the snake into the can. And closed the can. But not putting the lid on so tight hit would be hard to get off. I didn't want to have to jerk hit whenever I pulled off that lid. Then again, real gently and slow, I lifted the can across my shoulder. I eased out of the barn lot and went around through the back of the pasture and crossed the road some seventy-five to eighty yards into the woods, easy as I could.

I almost crept through the scope of woods, step by step to the back of the tabernacle. Didn't want to catch nobody's eye. That snake begun to move, and then I could hear hit swish-swishing. I kept on a-going.

Then I stepped inside the tabernacle.

They was faces and bodies as far as I could see, and right away all eyes was on me. Not a sound. Nowheres.

You ever stand alone before a big crowd? Everbody quiet, and staring at you? Hit'll scare you frazzling.

And, of course, there in front was all them deacon honchos of First Sanctified, solemn as Solomon. And right smackdab in the middle of them fine guests, setting there rared back, legs spread, and with one hand on each knee was guess who?

Uncle May and Aunt Josie was setting in chairs each side of the pulpit, looking straight ahead. I walked to the side of Uncle May.

I leaned over.

"Uncle May," I whispered. "I'm here."

He stayed setting there, stiff and quiet as that wood Indian in front of the cigar store over at the county seat. "Uncle May, Uncle May, I'm ready." Still nothing moved.

Had to do something.

I held the can under one arm and reached under his right arm with the other hand. Lifted him up. Oh-h-h, so—easy—and—gentle-like.

His arms went straight out like a jack handle with springs. His eyes walled back. "Kum see, kum si, kum tolly i—"

Real easy I lifted the can over right next to him and stood far back's I could get. I pulled on the lid, easy as I could, but hit didn't come loose just then like I meant hit to. Oh-h, lord.

I pulled harder. I heard that snake whishing and thrashing.

The lid had got looser. Pulled agin. Out the lid come.

And out the coral come.

Hit wriggled out the can onto, then over, Uncle May's shoulder.

Quick as greased lightning, hits rings all a blur, hit wrapped hitself around Uncle May's right arm, unwrapped hitself, wrapped around again.

Then hit just dropped off onto the ground.

Uncle May taken a rigor and down he went, his head busting into the side of the pulpit. From the crowd one big gasp.

Then quiet.

Silence. Real quiet.

But then come some shouts.

"Where's the snake?"

"Where's the moccasin?"

"Liar!"

Things was spinning so, hard to remember what all happened. I knowed we bad needed to get gone. Was I dreaming? Or crazy? Had I heard a shotgun blast over about the house? Aunt Josie and me both was trying to raise Uncle May up. He was dead weight. The last of my worries just then was how wet his britches was. I went to rubbing him and slapping his face. "Git up! Git up, Uncle May!"

Josie was down on her knees aside him bawling, "Oh, Lord, what have I done? Is he bit? Please, dear

Lord, please don't let him be bit! Dear Lord, please forgive me! Oh why didn't I tell him? Precious Jesus, please don't let him be bit!"

That crowd was gettin to be somethin else. I heard "Fraud!"

"LIAR!"

"FRAUD!"

Old Spode was one who shore knowed to act when the iron was hot. I seen him jump up, strike out, and vault hisself over the rail like a circus orangutan. He wasn't looking at me. He wasn't looking at Aunt Josie.

He wasn't even looking at Uncle May.

His eyes was past us.

That coral was wriggling and a-knocking up little dust bubbles, hits rings blurry, almost to the back edge of the tabernacle, and headed fast as it knowed how to out towards the woods.

Spode loped past it.

Then he turned and with that big foot of his'n kicked hit back into the tabernacle.

That snake coiled.

Hits tail balled around. Hit looked like hit had a head on both hits ends.

"This ain't nothin' but a worm!"

All eyes was on Spode. "Hit ain't even good white perch bait!"

He really was almost laughing. Then he reached down.

And, just as me and Josie both sung out,"DON'T!," up he snatched that coral.

"I'm fixin' to pinch hits head o—, o—"

Funny, ain't hit, how things come in flashes?

'Cause just then, and for one split second, a look come on his face what told you Kato Spode knowed what he had just did was awful dumb.

Then, quick as a flash again, still another look come on him let you know Spode knowed he had larned more in that *next* second than all the rest of his life put together.

He swang his arm up over his head and with a sweep slang hit down towards the ground. That snake stayed coiled around his wrist. Then he taken his other hand and stripped hit off. Spode grabbed his bit hand and went to stomping.

Sounds come out of him what split the bark off them post oaks.

Folks over at the county seat still swear they heard him yell.

They also say Uncle May preached the best funeral they ever heard.

But wope, about to get ahead of myself.

First off, me and Josie and Jim Hugh had done grabbed Uncle May, lifted, toted, and dragged him out the back of the tabernacle. Things still all a-swirling. Hollering.

"Brother Spode!" "What done happened with Brother Kato?" Spode was hopping, stomping, slinging his hand, and words coming out of him what shore wasn't no preacher words.

Uncle May was sort of waking, and us half dragging and him half walking. "Josie, this too slow! We gotta bring him to! Gotta git to the house first and douse him, or we ain't gon ever get to that car!"

"Jim Hugh, quick, go git that bucket outten the kitchen and git us some cool water from the well. Me 'n Josie'll come along with Uncle May."

Jim Hugh ran on ahead, and about the time I seen him hit the top step, I heard him hollering.

"Shit fire! Shit! Fire!"

"Jim Hugh! What you—!"

Them's . . . his guts!"

Jim Hugh was kinda sputtering and looking wobbly. And I soon seen why.

Buster Tate was laying out in the hall, pale as lard. Just below his belt a hole the size of my fists was blowed through his trousers. They was blood and pieces of flesh splattered on the floor and hall wall. Green blowflies was buzzing all around, going in and out that hole.

Then Josie seen it, too.

"Oh, my God!"

Uncle May didn't see air thing, of course. Josie had left him kinda leaning on the porch, and he was still standing out there with a dazed look on his face, not really making sense of what was going on.

"I done throwed water on the gasoline." Hit was Mr. Rodney, come up from the back room.

Soon as I heard the word "gasoline," I realized I was

smelling gas, and I seen the gas can turned over and matches scattered from a nickel box laying there. A five- or six-foot-wide puddle of gas, water, and skims of blood was all running together on the hall floor.

"Somebody take my truck now and git him to the doctor. And call the sheriff. I'm goner wait here." Mr. Rodney said hit in a ordinary kinda way, and Jim Hugh headed straight out to that panel truck, and glad to go, too.

Buster Tate's eyes was half shut, glazed over like eyes on one them dead rabbits. But ever little bit one of his arms would take a jerk. He wasn't dead. Not quite.

"I was setting in this rocker here in the bedroom," Mr. Rodney told the sheriff. "I seen Buster and Luster out front. Luster stayed there at the gate lookin' around. Buster come on in the hallway with that can of gas in one hand and that there box of matches in t'other. He begun pourin' gas all round. I eased up out the rocker but Buster seen me through this door. I'm sure he seen the shotgun too because he told me, 'You ain't got the guts to.'

"I told him, 'Ef you go to strike one match, I'm fixin' to see yours.'

"He did and I done what I told him."

"What about Luster?" the sheriff asked.

"He turned the fan on."

TWENTY-SIX

Stock's got to be fed. Cows got to be milked. Eggs gathered. Things got to go on. They's also times a man needs a boot, too. I unplugged the jug, taken myself a good snort, put the jug back in the crib corner. Felt hit going all the way down to my belly.

I was closing the crib door, turned around and there was Josie.

"You told me to tell him," she said.

Crossed my mind then she'd knowed all along what I'd always kept in back of that crib.

"And I done wrong not to."

"Josie, remember what Mama ustersay? 'Even the good Lord don't try to change somethin' what's already happened.'"

She was crying, sobbing mostly.

"Look, Josie, you showed more sense than me. Have you stopped and figgered out just how much better shape we in simply 'cause you *didn't* tell him? You look here. Listen at me! Where you think we'd be ef you had? All we'd have left of this house'd be them brick chimneys. And we'd all be hidin' out in some fish camp over in the Delter."

"I cain't help feelin' the way I do."

"Well, forgit it!"

"Hit ain't that easy, Hershell. You know that."

"Course it ain't, but do it anyways."

"Worser still is the reason I done it."

I knowed somehow not to ask her to tell me, then or ever. "Hush, Josie! You gotta put all this behind you. Forgit it, I tell you!"

She stood there. "And they's somethin' else."

"I bet I know, but what?"

"Not tellin' him now that I knowed."

"Don't never tell him that, neither."

"I done decided that."

I can tell you they's things you know you oughta—or ought not—to do, though you never will know just why you knowed hit.

I also seen then what hit taken to be a great lady. Hit ain't bein' perfect. Nawsiree. Not by a long shot.

That liquor had hit me 'cause then I done something I never had even thought of before. I wrapped both my arms around her and give her a bear hug.

"We Mooneyhams," I said.

We stood there together. Then she stepped back, looked at me, laughing and crying all at the same time: "Hershell, you remember what you said that dictator in Germny's name was?"

"Why shore. Rudolph Hillter. That ain't right?"

"Naw, hit's Rudolph *Hitler*, silly."

I thought it the best time right then to get something off my mind what had been there a long time. "Josie, I been studyin'. Things goner pick up now for you and the kids, I believe. I want to go back home."

"Home? Home?"

"Yeah. Back home."

She went to crying again. "Hershell, you air home. Don't you see that? And hit wouldn't be home to us ef you wasn't here."

TWENTY-SEVEN

Uncle May, Aunt Josie, me and the boys and Mr. Rodney was all in the courtroom when they wheeled Buster in, in a wheelchair.

He had one them great big family Bibles what covered his lap. Mr. Sam Hamman was his lawyer.

"How you plead?" Judge Taylor asked him.

"He pleads guilty, your honor," Mr. Hamman said. "And I would like to ask the court for mercy."

"Proceed, Mr. Hamman."

"As your honor knows, as things turned out, nobody was hurt here but Buster Tate hisself. He's the only one."

The judge told him he didn't see where that outcome was exactly Mr. Tate's plan.

"Thats right, your honor, but Jedge, I am sure your

honor has read the doctors' reports about my client. Parlized from waist down, legs might's well be rubber. This man ain't never gon walk one step rest of his life. And when his bowels move, won't be like your'n nor mine, but in a sack next to his belly. What good is hit sendin' him to Parchman? He couldn't be no worse off. Already been punished bad as a man can be."

"That may be true, Mr. Hamman," the judge said. "But the law is the law. I cannot think of anything more sneaking or lowdown than what this man was about to do if he had not been stopped by Mr. Massengill. Burning down the dwelling house of a minister of the gospel and his wife and little boys. A man what'd do that's too sorry to breathe."

Then the judge turned to Buster and said, "Just what kind of human being are you, do what you done?"

"My pastor's reason I done it," Buster broke in.

"Well, your pastor's not around to say if he had anything to do with what you done or not, but anyways, even if he did, you think that's any excuse for what you done? No excuse atall. Mr. Tate, you are hereby sentenced to the state pententry in Parchman for a term of ten years. That's the most I can give you under the law. He's in your custody, Mr. Sheriff."

Wheelchair turned and the bailiff started wheeling Buster out the courtroom. Looked like Buster was trying to look holes through somebody. I turned and seen Mr. Rodney staring right back. When they got even to where Mr. Rodney was setting, Buster grabbed the wheels to a stop.

"Whyn't you just go on and kill me?" Buster asked him.

"Whyn't you?" Mr. Rodney answered.

There's a warrant out for him, but nobody has heard hide nor hair of Luster.

TWENTY-EIGHT

I 'spect you'll be glad to know now, finally, I'm just about through.

Nobody on earth, including Josie even, knows Mayfield Yancy better'n me. Still—and this may sound funny to you—I cain't help feeling somehow that you—you done taken all this time setting there listening at me—you probly know him about as well as me. You can only go so far understanding that man.

Thinking back, seems like half the county was there that day, and the whole county sure knowed all about hit the next. Never heard such talk. "The Lord taken a lil ole snake you could of baited a catfish hook with and filled that thing with pizen." "The Holy Spirit smote Brother Yancy and whilst he was layin' there on the ground that snake crawled right up next to his ear. Looked like hit was tryin' to give him a message."

They had that snake all kinds of colors: brown, yellow, red, blue, white, some said striped, some said speckled. One said after hit bit Brother Spode, "Hit just stood up on hits tail, all stiff." Then, "like a invisble hand movin' a pencil, hit just floated out the back." Them tales got wilder'n wilder.

As you might guess, things changed now. Oh, my, how they have. When folks see him, they act like the Prince of Whales or the governor, even, just walked up. Everbody stops talking. Waiting to see what *the Preacher* got to say. Then swallowing in ever word.

Hit's "Brother Mayfield, we're fryin' two our fattest fryers for dinner Sunday. We'd be so pleased to have you, Miss Josie, and the boys eat with us." Or, "Brother Yancy, please come eat supper with us Satday night. We gon have chicken pot pie and dumplins."

Hit's "Brother Mayfield" this, and "Revrend Yancy" that all time. Nobody cain't get enough of him. *Everbody* all time bragging on him. (Only quiet folks them First Sanctified deacons.)

The church ladies have did a lot of private talking to Josie, too. One t'other them Sanctified sisters what wouldn't of come in a mile of her eight weeks back makes hit a point to let Josie know how *she* knowed all along Kato Spode was no good, or how low-down mean and stinkin' dirty he was, and how *she* always knowed Spode never preached Jesus and him crucified, but money and that multiplied. And what a blessing he's gone now.

On and on. You'd never know them sisters was speaking about the same man that a few weeks before was their pastor. Some of their old men—Ben Starr, Mat Drudge, and Wirt Beard—also had their say, privately, to Josie about Spode's sneaking meanness, and how thankful they are for all Brother Mayfield's done. All pure "d" palavering, ever bit of it. Ain't never heard such.

So here them Halls Siding Sanctifieds has went and gone from Kato Spode to Mayfield Yancy—and this here is religion? What'd that fool say that day, "one empty room after another"? In a crazy way right he was again, but shore different from what all he was a palavering about. Wasn't hit? Him and old Spode, that pair shore done something to whatever religion I had onct.

Say, you ever thought how humans are like weeds? That's right, weeds. Weeds. One way, shore ain't much about us to be proud of. Another, come hell or high water, no matter, wherever they are at, seems like humans and weeds are gonna stay here. I ain't got no business saying this. Naw, I ain't gonna say hit. Well, yes I am. Somehow I wonder why when the good Lord made us He decided not do a better job.

Mr. Oscar made a trip from the county seat all the way out to the house just to bring a letter, marked "SPECIAL DELIVERY" to "The Reverend Mayfield Yancy, Esquire." Some college in Oklahoma had wrote him to come out there to be a professor. He gonna get such a big head a louse'd swim a Lysol river to get on it.

But the dangdest get-out of all to me is I do believe hit's even turned Josie's head. Yesterday she told me, "Ain't he just, well—GRAND!"

But I ain't no idiot. And *I'm* still a Mooneyham like I told you first off. This ain't gonna last. No way. Something's gonna happen. He's walking around in a big old bubble just waiting to bust. Kersplatt. Wide open. For sure.

'Cause I know he ain't got a lick of sense, not brain one. I know he ain't. I know that for absolutely sure. I know.

By the by, why is a nail harder'n wood?

ACKNOWLEDGMENTS

The family of Armis Eugene Hawkins is extraordinarily grateful for the guiding hand of Ellen Douglas—Jo Ayers Haxton—for her encouragement, enthusiastic interest, and her keen insight. Armis remembered Jo Ayers from their childhood in Natchez and later from Professor Hutcherson's writing class at Ole Miss. But it would be many years later, when Armis served on the state court, that they became friends. He got much pleasure from the afternoons he spent talking politics and literature with Jo on her Belhaven porch.

We wish to thank our dear friend Mike Mills for his kind personal remarks and superb biographical essay.

In addition, we are truly appreciative of Carol Cox for her sensitive copyediting; Dale Hawkins Carr for her expressive sketch of "Uncle Armis" and her humorous drawing of our mule; Patti Henson for the jacket art; and artist Lea Barton for her continued inspiration and support.

Finally, we graciously thank and acknowledge Jo-Anne Prichard Morris for her diligence in ensuring that Armis' "little yarn," *The Grand Leader*, not remain lost in a dusty bin in the archives.

Pat, Janice, Jean Anne, and Jim
August 2007